A great weight pressed into Lucy's chest, restricting her breathing.

The instant photograph was small, only a few inches square, and the colors were bleached. The two grainy forms in the foreground were barely distinguishable as her and Jordan. Despite the poor quality, there was no mistaking the content. The picture was of the two of them, and had been taken outside her sunroom only moments before.

"I checked the angle. It looks like someone took the picture from your neighbor's yard. Are you certain you didn't leave that window open when you left this morning?" Jordan asked.

"Positive."

Jordan tapped his index finger against the steering wheel. "Whoever planted the listening devices probably left the window open as a bit of insurance for easy access to the house when necessary."

"Do you think they know we discovered the surveillance?"

"Even if they did, I don't think they care. They want you to know you're being monitored. Someone took the picture from the neighboring yard, then slipped it through the open wind ow while we were just... want you to feel on ed...

"It's working."

Sherri Shackelford is an award-winning author of inspirational books featuring ordinary people discovering extraordinary love. A reformed pessimist, Sherri has a passion for storytelling. Her books are fast paced and heartfelt with a generous dose of humor. She loves to hear from readers at sherri@sherrishackelford.com. Visit her website at sherrishackelford.com.

Books by Sherri Shackelford

Love Inspired Suspense

No Safe Place
Killer Amnesia
Stolen Secrets

Love Inspired Historical

Return to Cowboy Creek
His Substitute Mail-Order Bride

Montana Courtships
Mail-Order Christmas Baby

Prairie Courtships
The Engagement Bargain
The Rancher's Christmas Proposal
A Family for the Holidays
A Temporary Family

Visit the Author Profile page at Harlequin.com for more titles.

STOLEN SECRETS

SHERRI SHACKELFORD

LOVE INSPIRED SUSPENSE
INSPIRATIONAL ROMANCE

LOVE INSPIRED® SUSPENSE
INSPIRATIONAL ROMANCE

ISBN-13: 978-1-335-72159-4

Recycling programs
for this product may
not exist in your area.

Stolen Secrets

Love Inspired
22 Adelaide St. West, 40th Floor
Toronto, Ontario M5H 4E3, Canada
www.Harlequin.com

Printed in U.S.A.

Peace I leave with you, my peace I give unto you:
not as the world giveth, give I unto you.
Let not your heart be troubled, neither let it be afraid.
—John 14:27

To Tina Radcliffe and Stephanie Dees.
Thanks for coming to Nebraska to visit me.
The weather is always that nice. Really.

ONE

Adjusting his tie, Jordan Harris checked his reflection in the mirrored glass window of the coffee shop. His civilian haircut camouflaged the crescent scar looping around his left ear, and the extra volume of his suit jacket concealed his weapon. Satisfied his appearance was squared away, he pushed open the door.

The comforting aroma of freshly brewed coffee enveloped him in a soothing air-conditioned cloud. A half-dozen people were scattered throughout the colorful airy space. Four females, one toddler and three males. Soft perimeter. No credible threats. These days, no place was entirely safe. Not even Omaha, Nebraska.

A woman with white-blond hair sat with her back to the door. A soft breeze ruffled the wavy chin-length strands, revealing vivid blue streaks hidden throughout the layers.

Lucy Sutton.

He stared, mesmerized for a moment, before returning to his senses. Trained in masking his emotions, Jordan worked for the National Security Agency. He was a modern-day spy in a digital world. He was good at his job, but there were times when he felt as though his life was comprised of nothing more than smoke and mirrors.

Lucy turned, and he lifted his hand in greeting. They'd texted. He'd seen her picture plenty of times, and he assumed she'd looked him up on social media. Recognition softened her blue-gray eyes, and she waved him over.

She wore a dark floral-print dress with an enveloping black sweater. By the time he maneuvered through the jumble of mismatched tables and chairs, she'd stood, the top of her head not quite clearing his shoulder. Her expressive storm-colored eyes took up most of the real estate on her pixie face.

"Jordan Harris?" she asked, her voice slightly husky.

"Lucy Sutton, right?" he replied, though he'd have recognized her anywhere.

They exchanged the awkward, cursory greeting of two people who shared nothing beyond a mutual tragedy.

"It's good to finally meet you in person," he said.

A little over a year ago, he'd been assigned to an isolated intelligence recon mission overseas along with Lucy's fiancé, Brandt Gallagher. During the endless hours of monotonous surveillance, Brandt had shared portions of Lucy's emails to entertain them. Knowing they were far from home and missing the familiar, she'd transformed even the most mundane daily activities into amusing anecdotes.

As the weeks passed, Jordan had looked forward to her witty observations and keen intelligence. Knowing that nothing would ever come of it, he'd even allowed himself to develop a harmless crush on her.

"Nice to see you, too," she said, her smile warm. "This must be quite a change of pace after being overseas."

"Not as much as you'd think." He tucked his hands into his pockets. "I can't tell you how sorry I am about Brandt. I should have spoken to you earlier, but I couldn't…"

Lucy held up one hand, her eyes welling with tears. "Don't apologize. They told me you'd been injured." She studied his face, as though searching for any lingering signs of the explosion that had permanently altered his hairline. "They didn't tell me how badly, though."

"Not bad." He was heartily sick of the traumatic brain injury protocol, and he'd had enough neurological scans to map out his brain ten times over. "Fully recovered."

"Brandt promised me the job was rarely dangerous."

"Normally, it's not. But we work in hostile places, and there's always a risk."

"I miss him." Her throat worked. "You knew him better than I ever did. You knew him longer. With his parents gone, they gave me his flag. It should have gone to—" Her voice broke.

"I miss him, too." Jordan took her elbow and guided her toward the table. "You were his fiancée. He'd have wanted you to have it."

She sank onto her chair. "Thank you."

"I can't imagine what you're going through," he said. "I appreciate you meeting me, considering…"

He'd felt a connection to her even though they'd never met in person before today. Maybe it was because he'd had a childhood friend with the same name. Though she was nothing like the kid he'd known in school, hearing the name *Lucy Sutton* automatically came with a sense of belonging.

"Every day is different, you know?" Lucy's smile was overly bright and there were dark circles beneath her eyes. "You were a good friend to him, and that means a lot."

A band of emotion squeezed his chest. She wouldn't be saying that if she knew the truth of her fiancé's death. They'd been on the verge of wrapping up their assignment when something—or someone—had blown their cover. A suicide bomber had targeted the hotel where they were conducting their surveillance.

Jordan had survived the blast. Brandt had not. That was all Lucy knew about that day. She didn't know the suicide bomber had discovered the intelligence equipment Jordan and Brandt had planted earlier. That part was classified.

Her gaze skittered away, and she motioned to a chair. "Sit. Would you like something to drink?"

"I'm good."

Lucy reached for her coffee. Despite the unusually mild spring weather, she clutched the warm cup. He glanced at her hand, and his breath hitched. His carefully prepared speech shattered into a thousand tiny pieces.

She followed his gaze. "I should probably stop wearing the engagement ring. It's sentimental, I suppose, because of, well, you know…"

"You, uh…" He cleared his throat. "You should do whatever feels right to you."

According to Brandt, his whirlwind courtship with Lucy had prevented him from proposing with a proper ring. Near the end of their assignment, Brandt had produced a box from a shockingly exclusive jeweler in Islamabad who catered to Saudi princes and Russian oligarchs.

The day of the bombing, Brandt had asked him to hold the ring. Jordan had thought it was lost in the blast until they'd returned it to him last month. Some sort of mix-up had occurred, and the ring had been sitting in storage for months. This morning he'd planned on presenting the ring to Lucy along with an apology for the delay, but she was already wearing an identical piece of jewelry.

Why?

Lucy glanced at the sparkling diamond. "We'd only been dating for six months when he learned he was being sent back into the field. He proposed to me the next day."

"He was a force of nature," Jordan said. Brandt was outgoing, irreverent and brash. Standing next to him meant standing in the shadows, like comparing a color photo to the negative. "Once he knew what he wanted, he went after it all the way. There was no one else like him."

"He was relentless, that's for sure." She wriggled her fingers, and the diamond facets caught the sunlight streaming through the windows. "The ring was a compromise. Everything happened so fast. We agreed to a long engagement. I figured if our relationship survived his time in Pakistan, we'd have a chance."

"I'm glad we could meet in person," Jordan

said, searching for a way to justify his presence because there was no obvious explanation for a duplicate ring. "I hope you weren't too surprised when I contacted you."

"I couldn't have been more pleased." Her tone was earnestly sincere. "Having heard so much about you from Brandt, I was looking forward to finally meeting you in person."

"He'd read your emails out loud sometimes. Nothing personal, mind you. Just the silly stories. They kept us going."

"Don't look so guilty," she admonished lightly. "Brandt told me. He couldn't keep a secret even if he wanted to."

The door swung open, and Lucy whipped around. The toddler he'd seen earlier waved at them with chubby fingers.

Lucy's shoulders sagged and his attention sharpened. He wasn't the only person at this meeting who was searching for credible threats.

"Is there something wrong?" he asked.

"Everything is fine." With trembling fingers, she tucked a strand of hair behind one ear. "I'm jumpy. Too much coffee, I guess."

His immediate concerns took a back seat to more pressing matters. Lucy was probably good at many things.

Lying wasn't one of them.

He carefully considered his next words. "The

National Security Agency is a family," Jordan prodded gently. "We look out for each other. We take care of each other. You're a part of that family now."

"It's nothing." Her gaze darted around the room. "It sounds absurd even to me."

Fear was an emotion he encountered often in his line of work, and Lucy was terrified.

"I deal with the absurd for a living. Try me."

"Brandt said you were easy to trust." She rubbed her knuckles against the worry lines creasing her forehead. "When you contacted me last week, it was like an answer to my prayers. I had this idea that if I said everything out loud, I'd see how perfectly ridiculous I'm being."

Jordan narrowed his gaze. "Then you haven't spoken with anyone else about what's on your mind? A friend? A family member?"

"No." She blinked rapidly. "I can't."

He kept his posture relaxed and easy though his thoughts were troubled. While on a previous assignment, he'd been informed that his stepsister was in a serious car accident. She'd been writing about a prolific serial killer when she'd discovered the murderer's identity. Instead of seeking Jordan's help, she'd tried to handle the situation on her own—with near-fatal consequences. He didn't want Lucy to feel the same way.

He wanted her to trust him. "Why don't you start at the beginning?"

Leaning forward, she tipped her coffee before quickly righting the cup. "I think someone is trying to frame me for a security breach at work."

Jordan blinked.

He'd expected her to confess that she was having financial difficulties or something mundane. "You develop software for drone technology, right?"

"Yes." She took a shaky sip of her coffee. "Drones are coupled with satellites, and I write code to ensure a secure uplink. It's a lot more complicated than that, but that's the simple version."

The fine hairs on the back of his neck stirred. Overseas, drones did a massive amount of heavy lifting. Any disruption risked the safety of American troops.

"How do you think you're being framed?" he asked.

"I was afraid you'd laugh at me or tell me I'm being paranoid." She pressed her knuckles against her red-rimmed eyes. "Thank you for taking me seriously. No one else— Never mind. Just…thank you."

Confessing her worries had released a floodgate of emotion. She was on edge, her distress barely in check. Though he wanted to comfort her, calm was contagious, and if he avoided mirroring her emotions, she was more likely to stay in control.

"Just tell me what happened," he urged, keeping his tone professional. "And we'll go from there."

She took a few deep, fortifying breaths, then nodded.

"There was a data breach in my department while I was on vacation." She hugged the edges of her sweater together. "Nothing major, but enough to make everyone on the executive floor nervous. I didn't think much about it until last Thursday. I was working late to catch up when someone on the cleaning crew mentioned that I'd been working after hours a lot. Only I hadn't been in the office for almost a week."

"And they were certain it was you?"

"Yes. That's what caught my attention." She lifted a strand of her platinum hair. "I don't exactly blend into a crowd. I might have written it off as a mistake, but the night security guard said something similar." Casting a surreptitious glance over her shoulder, she whispered, "I think someone is impersonating me."

All of that was suspicious but not necessarily proof. "Anything else?"

"A barista at a coffee shop near the building where I work also mentioned seeing me."

"How well do you know the barista?"

"Not at all. I only stopped there because I was running late that day. It was the first time I'd ever been in that shop."

Possible explanations buzzed through his head. A doppelgänger was bizarre, yet not necessarily outside the realm of possibilities. Selling classified information was lucrative, but extremely risky for both the buyer and seller. Deflecting the blame created a tactical advantage.

"Have you informed your supervisor?" he asked.

"Informed him of what?" She splayed her hands. "That someone who looks like me parked their car in the lot and entered the building? How do I prove it *wasn't* me?"

She had a point. Depending on the clarity of the cameras and how well the impostor resembled her, there might not be a way to tell the difference.

"What do you know about the data breach?" He shifted directions. "What were they after?"

"I don't know. No one is talking." She ducked her head. "I think they're watching me. There's a chance my phone has been tapped. I even thought a car was following me today. Anything is possible."

That was an understatement.

She had no idea the sorts of surveillance that were possible these days, even for civilians. "The car you thought was following you—do you know the make and model?"

"A white sedan. Like a Toyota Corolla or something similar." She snapped her fingers. "There's something else. I got a couple of weird texts. They didn't make any sense, so I figured it was a wrong number."

"Do you still have them?"

"No. I deleted the thread. Like I said, I thought they were a mistake until the other stuff started happening."

He didn't believe in coincidences. Nearly a year ago, he'd lost his friend and colleague to a suicide bomber. This morning he'd discovered Brandt, with no apparent logical motivation, had lied to him about an engagement ring. He'd also learned that Lucy was the possible target of a frame-up.

That was one too many odd occurrences for his peace of mind.

"If what you suspect is true," Jordan began, "and someone is impersonating you to steal information, then you're at risk. You need protection."

He'd promised to look out for Lucy if anything ever happened to Brandt, and he'd already failed in that duty. He should have contacted her sooner, but he'd been a coward.

He'd been avoiding this meeting, hoping his feelings had faded. She'd been through enough already. She was vulnerable, and he wasn't going to take advantage of her. He owed that much to Brandt. Being near her would be punishing; maybe she was the penance he deserved.

"Never mind." Lucy twisted around, reaching for the voluminous leather tote hanging on the back of her chair. "Forget I said anything. I'm sure it's all a mistake anyway."

Jordan absently touched his breast pocket, then decided against saying anything. He didn't know what the second ring meant, and there was no reason to upset her. Until he knew otherwise, he was dedicated to preserving Brandt's memory. He'd be loyal in his actions if not his feelings.

"Lucy—"

His next words froze on the tip of his tongue. Through the coffee shop window, he saw a white sedan appear. The unmistakable glint of a gun barrel caught his attention. Jordan's training kicked into action, and he launched himself over the table to protect Lucy.

At Jordan's swift movement, Lucy startled. The glass pane at the front of the shop exploded.

Time slowed and Jordan caught hold of her. Shards of glass showered over them, clattering to the floor like a hailstorm. He dragged her down, and they both tumbled over her chair. She braced for a painful landing, but he angled his body at the last minute, taking the worst of the blow. The jolt knocked the air from her lungs.

A woman screamed, and a table crashed near Lucy's head. Someone was shooting at them.

Voices sounded in panic from all directions, and she struggled to make sense of the commotion. Jordan kept her anchored in place, and she instinctively fought the restriction. Adrenaline pumped through her veins, urging her into fight-or-flight mode.

"I need a better vantage point," he whispered roughly, retrieving a gun from inside his jacket. "Stay down and out of sight. I'll let you know when it's safe to move toward the exit."

A loud bang was followed by a dusty spray of plaster.

Without giving her a chance to protest, Jordan moved away.

When she reached for him, her fingers closed around air.

Several customers cowered behind tables while others crouched in place. Everyone was frozen in terror. She had to think. She'd gone through active shooter training at work. Human

Resources had been relentless in drilling the instructions. *Run first, hide if necessary, fight back as a last resort.*

A dark-haired woman in a bright yellow shirt crouched near the front of the shop, her hands covering her ears. Another pop sounded, and glass rained over the woman's head. She screamed and rocked back and forth.

Fight or flight. Fight or flight. Fight or flight.

The words echoed like a mantra through Lucy's head. Her vision wavered.

Flight.

"Stay low," Jordan shouted. "Get to the back of the store."

"This way!" Lucy called to the woman in yellow. She gestured toward the service counter. She'd seen workers entering from the back on numerous occasions. "There's an exit through the kitchen."

The woman crawled a few feet, her movements jerky and uncoordinated.

The top pane of the front door burst into a thousand tiny shards. Lucy flattened her body and covered her head. Paralyzed by the terror pumping through her veins, her hands tingled.

"Please, God," Lucy begged, "give me strength."

In an attempt to contain her fear, she focused on the woman in yellow. "You're doing great. Keep going. You're almost there."

Their eyes locked, and Lucy saw her own horror mirrored in the woman's gaze. The reality of their situation nearly undid her, and she fought for control.

"Get to the exit!" Jordan shouted.

"What about you?"

"I'm right behind you."

She peered cautiously from behind her shelter. He'd positioned himself at the front of the store, his gun drawn. Given Brandt's praise of him, she had no doubt he'd sacrifice his life to prevent the shooter from coming through that door. He was offering himself as a shield to let them escape.

Another bullet ripped over her head, shattering a picture on the back wall. Lucy screamed. Tears blurred her vision. Though she was reluctant to leave Jordan behind, she didn't want his sacrifice to be in vain. The woman in yellow had reached the relative safety of the service counter. She had a clear path to the exit.

As Lucy belly-crawled in her wake toward the kitchen, she encountered a man in a suit crouched behind the service counter. He jabbed at his phone, his hands trembling wildly. She navigated through the broken glass, her sweat-slicked palms hindering her progress.

"Go," she ordered. "Run. Get out."

A bullet blasted a hole in the back wall. Lucy yelped.

"I don't want to die." The man's eyes were wild and unfocused. He gripped her arm in a painful vise, trapping her in place. "Don't leave me."

The stranger's terror sparked a hidden reserve of strength within Lucy, and a precise sort of clarity took hold of her thoughts. Panicking only exacerbated the situation.

Prying the man's fingers from her arm, she said, "Stay calm and exit the building."

The words sounded trite considering the situation, but they worked. She touched his shoulder. The contact was like a spark of lightning, and the man jumped.

"Okay," he said, then scrambled toward freedom.

His movement lifted the stark paralysis of the four remaining customers, who'd been rooted in place. It was as though someone had given them permission to act. In a crowded scramble, they dashed toward the exit. Lucy followed in an awkward, crouching run. Another shot burst through the menu hanging above the counter. She pivoted and twisted her ankle. The next step was agony and she dropped to her knees.

The hanging lamp above her head exploded, and a white-hot flash of pain burst through her cheek. With a startled shriek, she cringed and curled into a ball. Her fear was so sharp she tasted it on her tongue.

She didn't want to die. Not here. Not now. Not like this.

"Please, God. Just a few more minutes," she prayed. "I just need a few more minutes of strength."

Mustering every ounce of fortitude to bolster her courage, she searched for Jordan. He'd sacrificed his own safety to let them escape. Where was he? He should be following them since everyone had exited.

The next instant there was silence. Complete, deafening silence. No gunshots. No voices.

Nothing.

The nothing terrified her more than the gunshots.

TWO

Lucy desperately searched for Jordan. Why had the gunfire stopped? Where was the shooter?

A buzzing sounded in her ears. She started toward the exit, but her muscles rebelled. Her limbs were heavy, and her blood moved sluggishly through her veins. A sticky lethargy dragged her into a dense fog.

"Lucy." Jordan scrambled toward her, though his voice seemed to be coming from a great distance. "It's clear. He won't be back. Not with the police on the way."

His brief, bone-crushing embrace cleared the haze, and she welcomed the pain.

Sitting back, he tucked two fingers beneath her chin. "You're hurt."

She touched the spot and her fingers came away red. "It's nothing."

Her hands were shaking, and she stared at them as though they belonged to someone else.

The faint wail of sirens sounded in the distance, and she nearly wept with relief.

Jordan stood and crossed to the counter, then returned with a handful of napkins. He pressed the crumpled wad against her cheek, and she winced.

"Sorry," he murmured.

She caught his concerned gaze, and her pulse tripped. Jordan was not the man she'd pictured in her head. The way Brandt had described him, she'd been expecting a doddering computer geek with a pocket protector, a horseshoe of thinning hair and a circle of white tape repairing the bridge of his glasses. The one grainy photo she'd managed to find on the internet had only hinted at the man crouched beside her.

Jordan did not wear glasses, and there was nothing doddering about him.

He was handsome.

Awareness jolted through her, and she shoved the unwelcome feeling aside. After the initial shock and grief of losing Brandt, she'd retreated into numbness. Feeling nothing was better than feeling the pain.

A teeth-rattling shiver traveled the length of her body. "I'm c-cold."

"Take this." Jordan shrugged out of his jacket and draped the material around her shoulders.

"The paramedics will check if you need stitches. Are you hurt anywhere else?"

"My ankle, I think."

"Let me take a look." He gently touched the slight swelling. "It's not too bad."

She glanced at her engagement ring, and her stomach clenched. Brandt had tumbled into her life with all the chaotic enthusiasm of a golden retriever puppy. He'd been warm and affectionate, passionate and quick-tempered. She'd been charmed, dazed and knocked for a loop. In her family, affection was reserved, and praise was tempered. With Brandt, everything had been overwhelming and captivating.

Her friends and family didn't understand her grief for someone she'd dated for only six months. They thought the engagement was rushed. They hadn't gotten a chance to know him before he traveled overseas. They hadn't gotten to read his emails and Skype with him. They hadn't gotten to see the two of them together beyond a few events and a hasty farewell party. But from the moment she'd seen Jordan this morning, she'd sensed he recognized the depth of her loss.

The sirens grew louder, and Jordan grimaced. "When the police get here, it'll be like someone kicked the ant bed. They'll swarm us. Don't make any sudden moves."

Lucy glanced at the clock. Not even two minutes had passed. That first shot had changed the course of so many lives in the blink of an eye.

"O-okay."

"You're in shock," he said, and she focused on his calm reassurance. "Take a few deep breaths. You'll be okay."

You'll be okay.

Such an odd thing to say. *Your fiancé is dead, but you'll be okay. Someone tried to kill you, but you'll be okay. Your world is falling apart around you, but you'll be okay.*

A deafening cacophony of emergency vehicles sent her head pounding. Tires screeched. Voices called. She was separating from herself, viewing the events from a distance, as though recalling a nightmare instead of living one. For the first time she noticed her cheek was throbbing. She'd been numb to the pain until now.

Her phone buzzed, and she automatically glanced down. A text alert flashed on the screen followed by a photo.

Someone had taken a picture of the shattered coffee shop window from the street.

A sense of horror enveloped her. A part of her had wanted to believe that she was connecting dots that weren't supposed to be connected. She had a vivid imagination, after all. She always had her head in the clouds.

"You did good back there," Jordan said, his words barely registering through the cloud of shock. "You didn't lose your cool."

Another message appeared. She blinked rapidly and the letters blurred at the edges. This threat was immediate and shockingly real.

Are you ready to meet?

A second photo appeared. The outside of her house. This wasn't the end.

This was the beginning.

Jordan paced.

The aftermath of the shooting was like watching a film of something exploding, then viewing that same film in reverse. Just as quickly as the gunman had thrown them into chaos, law enforcement had arrived and gathered the pandemonium into a crude sort of order.

Everyone had a task. Everyone had something to do. Everyone but Jordan.

As the time ticked away, he paced. He scowled. He glanced at his phone for the hundredth time.

Playing the role of patient bystander was outside of his skill set.

An older, heavyset cop approached him. "You Jordan Harris?"

"That's me."

"You can see your wife now."

Jordan started. "Lucy?"

The cop frowned. "You got more than one wife?"

"Nope. Uh, lead the way."

There'd be time enough to sort the details later. Knowing Lucy was in danger had taken a decade off his life.

Perched on a stretcher in the back of the ambulance, she had a bandage on her cheek, and the paramedics had wrapped her ankle. To his relief, she appeared exhausted but otherwise not seriously harmed.

The officer glanced between them. "The detective in charge is finishing up with another witness. He'll speak with you both as soon as he can."

The older cop turned away.

A black SUV with tinted windows pulled into the parking lot, and Jordan stowed his phone. Local law enforcement wasn't going to be pleased about having their jurisdiction usurped, but this was a matter of national security.

He reached for Lucy. "Let's go."

"Wait… What?" She gestured with her thumb. "Aren't we supposed to stay?"

"Nope." He glanced at her ankle. "Can you walk?"

"I, uh… I think so. Maybe."

He reached for her, letting his hands hover near her shoulders. "This will be easier if I carry you. Are you okay with that?"

"I guess, but I'm too heavy."

He scooped her into his arms.

At the feel of her, a shock ran through his arms and landed with a sizzle in his chest.

"Don't worry," he said. "I've got a Bowflex."

Lucy chuckled. "You're kidding."

"I'm very manly." Her laughter warmed him, and one edge of his mouth kicked up. "I also chop wood and jog uphill carrying sacks of concrete mix."

She looped her arms around his neck. "Now I know you're pulling my leg."

He didn't mind adding a touch of levity to the moment. No one had been seriously injured. They were alive. Given the past few months, there hadn't been many light moments for either of them.

As they approached the SUV, the driver's door swung open. An agent whose name escaped Jordan's memory unfolded from his seat.

"Agent Harris, we met once before." The man opened the rear door. "I'm Luke Westover."

Jordan mentally snapped his fingers. Westover had the sort of Midwestern captain-of-the-football-team good looks that guaranteed a "swipe right" on the dating apps. They'd met during a briefing in Pakistan the previous year.

The agent leaned toward Lucy and handed her an ice pack. "From the EMT."

"Thank you," she replied with a shy smile.

Jordan cast a sharp glance at her, but she appeared oblivious to the agent's appeal. Not that it was any of his business. Lucy could admire whomever she pleased. Jordan was protective of her, that was all. As a friend. While Westover was a good agent, he also had all the sensitivity of a toddler in a ball pit. She deserved better, that was all.

"Let's get out of here before the press descends," said a familiar voice from behind him.

Howard Karp slipped into the passenger seat, leaving Jordan to take the spot next to Lucy.

Karp was in his late fifties with graying hair and the kind of trustworthy face that sold reverse mortgages on late-night TV. He had five identical suits in his closet, one for each day of the week.

He stared at them over a pair of wire-rimmed glasses perched on his bulbous nose, then stuck out his hand and introduced himself to Lucy. "Apologies in advance. We need to get ahead of this thing quickly." His gaze dipped to her leg and the ice pack she was pressing against her ankle. "Consider yourself in protective custody."

Lucy swallowed. "Okay."

"We'll keep your name out of the press. The next few days are going to be busy. Is there anyone you need to call? Parents? Friends?"

"Uh, no. Not if it's only a few days. But I need to call my work."

"I'll take care of that. We'll send an agent by your house to pick up a few things."

"No." Lucy vigorously shook her head. "I need to go myself."

"Not a good idea," Jordan said. "We can't risk exposure. Someone followed you this morning. There's a chance they're watching your house."

"I need to go home," Lucy said with a stubborn tilt of her chin. "They had a chance to kill me today and they didn't. They can't afford to. They need something from me."

Jordan exchanged a glance with Karp.

She was smart—he couldn't fault her for that. "Okay. We'll separate into two vehicles, and only one of us will accompany you inside."

"I got this one," Westover announced from the front seat. "I'll take her."

"No." A fierce possessiveness gripped Jordan. "This one is mine."

He clenched his back teeth together. A standup guy didn't let himself have feelings for his friend's girl. There were unwritten rules. Jordan was alive because one of the hotel's stone pillars had deflected the worst of the shrapnel. He was here with Lucy when Brandt should have been. Lucy needed a friend and a protector. This was about loyalty, not about his personal feelings.

"We'll swing by your house, then." Karp adjusted his glasses. "Can I get a look at the messages you received following the shooting?"

Lucy handed her phone over the seat.

"It's from a burner account, I'm guessing." Karp stared at the screen. "But we'll check it out anyway. Local police are pulling all the surveillance footage from nearby businesses. If that doesn't pan out, we'll widen the net and canvass for doorbell cameras."

"Even if you find something, it's going to be useless," Jordan said. "This guy was icy. Seven shots, fifteen seconds apart. All aimed above sight line."

"A warning?"

"An order," Jordan replied grimly, recalling the information he'd gathered. "We need to learn everything we can about the person who tried to access the information from Lucy's employer, Consolidated Unlimited. I'll contact her supervisor and see what they were after. I'll also pull the security footage. Sounds like someone tried to impersonate her."

Lucy stifled a yawn.

She caught his gaze and her cheeks flushed.

"I don't know what's wrong with me. I'm exhausted all of a sudden."

"It's the shock," Jordan said. "If you can, close your eyes. It helps."

"That seems impolite, somehow." Her eyelids drooped and she rubbed her cheeks. "It's like the adrenaline wore off and took all my energy with it."

"It's a common feeling." Jordan gave a rueful laugh. "You were shot at this morning—you don't have to worry about being rude."

There was no way to predict how the brain might react to stress. People generally responded to shock in one of two ways—either they became jumpy and hyper, or exhausted and drained.

Lucy covered her mouth, her nostrils flaring as she stifled another yawn. "I used to get carsick as a kid. The medicine my parents gave me knocked me out. It's like I'm conditioned to fall asleep when I'm in the back seat."

The ice pack forgotten, she turned slightly, curled her uninjured leg beneath her and rested her cheek against the back of the seat. Jordan shifted. He was too cramped to get comfortable. Westover had jammed the driver's seat as far back as the vehicle allowed, crowding Jordan's knees.

Road construction had narrowed the highway

to one lane, and a mile of headlights extended into the distance. Jordan angled his body to buy himself some leg room and stretched his arm across the seat.

Slowed to a crawl, Westover made annoyed noises and slapped his palm against the steering wheel. Karp kept his attention focused on a sheaf of papers in his lap. The minutes stretched out in silence and the hum of the engine was strangely soothing after what they'd been through that morning.

Soon Lucy's breathing grew deep and even. Jordan wasn't quite sure how it happened, but the next thing he knew, she was nestled into the crook of his arm. Conscious of his audience, he stiffened, but there was nowhere to go. Instead, he forced himself not to notice the soft brush of her hair against his skin or the way her head nestled perfectly in the nape of his neck. He ignored the jolt of awareness when she splayed her hand against his chest.

Karp swiveled in his seat. "Let her sleep. She's still got a long day ahead of her."

Westover's curious gaze appeared in the rearview mirror. "Anyone else think it's odd that her fiancé was killed and now someone is taking potshots at her?"

"Yeah." Jordan's gut twisted. "It's worth a second look."

The day of the bombing had started like any other. They were about to wrap up their surveillance, and Jordan was restless. Sometimes that happened at the end of a job. Sitting in the same room day after day, week after week, didn't bother him until he knew it was almost over. That was when the walls started closing in around him.

Brandt had understood. He'd urged Jordan to visit the local market. It was their third assignment together, and he knew that Jordan always picked up something for his dad before going home.

Grab a silk scarf for me, will you? Jordan recalled the last words Brandt had said to him. *Something with embroidery. Lucy's favorite color is blue.* Wanting to select the perfect shade, Jordan had lingered over the task.

"Everything about this is odd," he muttered into the heavy silence. "Why target Lucy in the first place?"

Seven years on the job and not one of his installations had ever been discovered. Not until that day. And Brandt had paid with his life. What had they done wrong?

"Was there anything odd before the bombing?" Karp asked. "Anything that might be connected?"

A faded scene tugged at the edges of Jordan's

memory. The night before, he'd seen Brandt speaking with a woman in the hotel lobby. When he'd interrupted them, Brandt had said she was visiting from out of town and needed some advice on where to eat. Except something hadn't rung true about the story.

Jordan shook his head to clear the memory. Was he reading into the chance encounter to assuage his own guilt?

"Maybe," he said with a glance at Lucy. "I'm not sure if it means anything. We can talk more later."

Karp adjusted his seat belt. "Here's our working theory based on what little we know so far. Someone impersonating Lucy made a deal and didn't deliver. Only the person on the other end of the deal—we'll call him the buyer—doesn't know he's been double-crossed. Which means he's pressuring the *real* Lucy to come through. Chances are, the fake Lucy has gone underground. Which means we have the perfect opportunity to set a trap."

"I know what you're thinking," Jordan said, unease skittering down his spine. Setting a trap meant leaving bait. "Not an option."

The duplicate engagement ring weighed heavily in his pocket. A second Lucy. A second ring. What other secrets were in store for them?

"It's the only way," Karp said quietly. "Either

you're with us, or I'll find someone else to take your place."

Lucy's platinum hair shimmered in the afternoon sunlight, and her subtle jasmine scent surrounded Jordan.

His head throbbed. "You know my answer."

He didn't like it—but there was no way he'd abandon her.

Because the only bait they had was Lucy.

THREE

Lucy stared at her kitchen counter. Something wasn't right.

She'd purchased the hundred-year-old house in a diverse area of town the year after she'd paid off her student loans. The compact two-story featured a living room, kitchen and sunporch on the first floor, along with two dormered bedrooms on the second floor. Real estate was an investment, or so she'd told herself. In truth, apartment living was claustrophobic, and she enjoyed gardening.

Jordan appeared in the doorway. "We don't have much time. Take only the essentials."

She hadn't been able to look him fully in the eye since waking in the car. What sort of person fell asleep in front of strangers? He'd handled the whole awkward encounter with brisk efficiency, but she hadn't felt such an acute sense of embarrassment since junior high.

The other agent, Westover, had tossed her a

speculative glance—which she'd ignored. He was probably wondering what Brandt had seen in someone like her.

She pictured the spouses at the NSA Christmas party as perfect carbon copies of each other—thin, expertly coiffed women with honey-blond hair, designer cocktail dresses and seats on the hospital fund-raising board. The kind of women Lucy's mom wanted her to emulate. When she'd said as much to Brandt, he'd laughed and said they didn't have an office Christmas party.

Pulling her attention back to the present, she concentrated on the black-and-white-checked tile of her kitchen floor. "I'll be quick."

Only a few hours had passed, but it might as well be an eternity. Everything was the same, yet everything felt different. Probably she was letting her imagination run away with her. Who could blame her after this morning?

The agents had taken great pains to ensure everything appeared normal. They'd retrieved her car from near the coffee shop, and Jordan had driven her here. Karp and Westover were parked around the corner in case someone was watching the house. Given the photo she'd received, they were right to be cautious.

Though she tried to convince herself otherwise, the sense of unease lingered.

"Something isn't right," she said, her gaze fixed on the far end of the room. "But I can't put my finger on what's out of place."

Jordan's posture changed ever so slightly. There was a sharpness to his gaze and his shoulders stiffened.

"It's probably nothing," he said casually, too casually for his shift in stance. "It's the stress. Messes with your head. You've been through a lot this morning."

Feeling as though she'd gotten the wrong notes for an important meeting, Lucy frowned. "Yeah. Stress."

Jordan stepped closer. "No place is safe these days."

She murmured something innocuous that was meant to signal her agreement.

If he was trying to warn her, there was no need. After this morning, she was well aware of the danger.

Hypervigilant now, she searched for the source of her unease.

With Jordan close behind her, she cautiously opened a kitchen drawer. "This isn't how I left things."

Reaching around her, he carefully pushed the drawer shut.

"I was just trying to help," he said, the heat of

his body close against her back. "Your system of organization is too complicated."

Instantly flustered, she struggled to make sense of his words. Jordan had never even been to her house, and he'd certainly never put away her dishes.

He held his index finger before his lips, then tapped his ear. Her breath caught. He thought someone was listening to them. Why hadn't the possibility occurred to her sooner? *Because I was a normal person before this morning, that's why*, she mentally reassured herself.

Jordan hoisted an eyebrow. "Don't you want to tell me why your system of organization makes perfect sense?"

He appeared to be running the conversation on autopilot, his attention clearly distracted.

"As a matter of fact, I do." Her heart pounded against her ribs. "You're supposed to organize by categories."

Backing away, he tilted his head. Though the ceilings were tall, he easily reached the smoke detector.

Using his fingertips, he gently unscrewed the cover. "How do you organize by categories?"

"It's really s-simple," she squeaked. Not only was Jordan searching for listening devices—he was finding them. "You start by putting everything from your kitchen into one big pile. Then you hold each item and decide if it makes you happy."

He tugged on a few wires and stepped back. "How do you know if something makes you happy?"

A tiny, round disk dangled from the plastic case. Her mouth went dry and she swayed, clutching the counter for balance. She was being monitored.

The past few weeks came into sharp focus, and nausea rose in the back of her throat. All the days and evenings she'd thought she was alone, someone had been with her. Someone had been shadowing her every move in the house.

What had she said? What had they heard?

Though she wanted to shout into the tiny microphone, she held herself in check. "You just know if something makes you happy, I guess."

As she recalled snippets of her inane chatter and off-key singing, hysterical laughter bubbled in the back of her throat. She sincerely hoped they'd been tortured by her screeching renditions of show tunes.

Jordan snatched a piece of paper from the kitchen island, and she scrambled to locate a pen.

"That sounds like quite a project," he said, then scribbled, *Just go along with whatever I say.*

The laughter died in the back of her throat. This was serious. Someone had followed her this morning. Shot at her. They knew where she lived. What else did they know about her?

Gazing in revulsion at the listening device, Lucy nodded her understanding of his instructions.

Jordan crossed into the living room and studied her bookshelf, then did a half circle. The walls were teal blue and plastered with colorful paintings she'd purchased at local art fairs over the years. Oriental rugs in deep shades of garnet and orange covered scratches in the ancient wood flooring. An original ornate chandelier dangled its crystal beads, and the sofa was covered in bright floral throws.

Her mom loathed this room. She claimed the mix of patterns exacerbated her migraines, and she was forever nudging the furniture into right angles.

Lucy squared her shoulders and studied Jordan's expression for any signs of judgment, then caught herself. She didn't care what he thought of her decorating. He didn't live here—she did.

Running his fingers along the top of her bookcase, he asked, "What happens if something doesn't make you happy?"

Her mind went blank. What on earth was he talking about? *Organizing.* They were talking about organizing. She'd make a terrible spy. Even as her perceptions of her safe, monotonous world were fragmenting around her, her thoughts drifted to the mundane.

Jordan dusted his hand against his pant leg, and Lucy cringed. "If something doesn't make you happy, then you get rid of it."

He moved several knickknacks, frowning at each one in turn. Why hadn't she curated her collection of bedazzled elephant figurines when she was organizing the kitchen? No, she was proud of her flamboyant style. It wasn't for everyone, sure, and maybe she wasn't the tidiest person in the world, but she wasn't a hoarder or anything awful like that.

Jordan removed and replaced each book. "What about me? Do I make you happy? Because you're going to be seeing a lot of me. Especially after what happened today."

He splayed his arms, urging her to agree.

"Absolutely you make me happy." This time she didn't hesitate. "You may stay."

If only putting the rest of her life in order was as simple as organizing the linen closet. What else might she excise that didn't make her happy? She'd start with traffic jams and finish with the person who was impersonating her.

"Excellent." Jordan stepped closer and spoke close to her ear. "Almost done. You're doing great." He raised his voice. "As usual, there's nothing to eat here. Why don't we go out?"

"Sounds good," she agreed, her stomach churning.

Food was the last thing on her mind. Momentarily at a loss, she took a few halting steps. The events of the day were starting to catch up with her, and she was having trouble focusing. A list of tasks bounced through her head. She needed to find someone to water her plants. She needed to check the locks. She needed…to feel safe again.

As though sensing her distress, Jordan's expression softened.

"Sit," he ordered gently. "Rest your ankle."

"It's better already." Her nerves were raw, and the pain was the furthest thing from her mind. "Hardly a twinge."

"I know you've had a long day, but I think it's better if we go out to eat. You could use a change of scenery."

"That would be nice," she replied with a nod to their invisible audience. She felt as though she was a marionette being coaxed into speaking. "I can walk as long as you go slow."

"Don't forget to grab your things. You shouldn't be here alone tonight."

Lucy widened her eyes. "Do we want people to know I'm leaving?"

If someone was listening, how much should they give away?

"You'll only be gone a few days." Jordan shrugged. "Just until the excitement dies down."

Her pulse hadn't returned to normal since she'd learned someone was listening to them. Even gathering an overnight bag seemed like an overwhelming task.

Lucy knotted her index finger in the hair at the nape of her neck. "Sorry about the mess."

Seeing her house through Jordan's eyes increased the tension. There were always stacks of books on the coffee table, and papers seemed to breed and multiply the moment she turned her back. There were a few dishes in the sink and more set to dry on the counter. Judging by the smudge on Jordan's pant leg, the whole place needed a good dusting.

"I like your place." He tweaked a patchwork throw on the back of a chair. "It's exotic. Like a Moroccan market."

She assumed he was merely being polite. What else was he going to say? *It looks like a circus clown threw up in your living room.* Then again, if this was how conversations played out when people were listening, she was tempted to tell her mom about the surveillance equipment. Maybe an audience would coax a compliment out of her. Lucy snorted. Not likely.

Jordan tilted his head. "Are you sure you're all right?"

His concern sent melting warmth through her

chest before she caught herself. Having him here brought back a torrent of emotion.

Jordan reminded her of a future she'd finally given up on. She missed Brandt. She missed his larger-than-life personality. She missed his understanding. She even missed his terrible taste in movies.

Lately she'd felt his memory slipping away, and letting go had felt like losing Brandt all over again. That was why it was easier to be numb. Except Jordan invoked a confusing mix of emotions she wasn't quite ready to face.

"I'm fine." Her head throbbed. "Still a little dazed, I guess. I'll get the rest of my things from upstairs."

Jordan reached for the paper and wrote, *Let me go first, just in case.*

Unable to speak, she nodded. Even going upstairs felt like an irrationally enormous undertaking.

The stairs were tight in the turn-of-the-century house, and Jordan had to duck his head.

Once upstairs, she relaxed a little. Her bedroom walls were a deep shade of salmon. A Turkish rug in a mix of magenta, orange and yellow covered the floor. Keyhole-patterned curtains blocked the late-afternoon sunlight.

She was running out of adrenaline, energy

and outrage. There was no way to go back and pay attention to the niggling unease that had been plaguing her for the past few weeks. Someone had been in her house. Someone had been watching her. All she could do was move forward with a solemn promise to be more vigilant in the future.

Jordan hovered politely outside the door while she gathered her belongings, and his calm, steady presence gave her the strength to continue.

She tossed a few items onto her patterned bedspread and paused. When had she started doubting her own taste? She enjoyed the blue streaks in her hair and her quirky wardrobe. She enjoyed standing out in a crowd. Yet, when she was alone with herself, the walls of her private life were a dull gray.

She sometimes wondered if she'd made herself unique by default because there was nothing inherently special about her. She sometimes wondered if Brandt would have gotten bored with her once the newness of their relationship had worn off.

The floorboards creaked in the hallway, and she quickened her pace. Without giving herself too much time to think, she stuffed clothing and toiletries into her overnight bag. The agents hadn't exactly been forthcoming about how long she was going to be away.

He surveyed the room with a critical eye, and her skin felt as though she'd brushed through cobwebs. A stranger had rifled through her personal belongings. They wouldn't have discovered anything beyond her utility bills and programming homework, but that didn't make her feel any less violated.

Jordan took the overnight bag from her stiff fingers and waved her forward. "We'd better get going. I'm starving."

"Me, too," she answered woodenly.

The full weight of her new circumstances settled over her, and she stumbled blindly after him. Had it not been for this morning, she doubted she'd have noticed anything out of place. She'd have continued along, blissfully ignorant that someone was listening to her, maybe even watching her. If this experience had taught her anything, it was that safety was an illusion.

On the first level once more, a scuttling sounded from the opposite end of the house.

Jordan shoved her behind him and drew his gun.

Her pulse spiked, and horror clouded her vision in a red haze.

She lunged before him. "Stop!"

Trapped between Lucy and a threat, Jordan's extensive training fought a losing battle with his instincts. He jerked his weapon safely to one side.

"Lucy!" he whispered harshly. "Get out of the way."

Her hair was a wild, pale halo framing her fierce expression, and she positioned herself like a miniature warrior before him.

"It's not what you think," she whispered loudly.

Jordan stuck out his hand. "I don't know what to think yet."

He was larger and stronger, but something kept him from forcibly moving her out of the way. If there was someone else in the house, there'd been ample opportunity to ambush them before now.

"It's just Mr. Nibbles," she declared.

Wavering, Jordan struggled to connect a logical meaning in her words. "Come again?"

"My guinea pig." Lucy indicated the smoke detector to remind him of their audience. "If we're going to be spending a lot of time together, you'll have to get better acquainted with Mr. Nibbles."

He stowed his gun, his shoulders losing some of their tension. "Your guinea pig is in the other room?"

"Yes."

Rather than reveal how ridiculous he felt, Jordan maintained a stoic expression.

"He's in the sunroom." Lucy crossed the distance. "He's the sweetest little thing in the world, but he gets nervous around strangers. That's why I have to fetch him myself."

"I see," he replied, even though he didn't.

He certainly didn't need instinct or training to recognize he was walking into some sort of trap. People tended to overestimate their pets' appeal to others. When someone followed the phrase *he's really the sweetest little thing* with a qualifying *but*, there was reason to be worried.

Willing his blood to cool, he followed her through the kitchen and into a cheery yellow sunroom.

There, perched on a low wooden table, was an enormous cage connected with clear plastic tubing to a smaller cage. Inside, a white guinea pig with brown markings contentedly gnawed on a half-eaten chunk of carrot. The animal's nose twitched, and if Jordan didn't know better, he'd have thought the furry little troublemaker was smirking at him.

"Oh, sweetie, are you all right?" Lucy cooed, lifting the animal from its cage.

Tired, hungry and ready for this day to be over, Jordan grumbled. Mr. Nibbles was annoyingly calm, considering Jordan had drawn his gun.

Lucy bent and rooted around in the cage. "He'll have to come with us. I can't leave him here alone." She crossed to Jordan and whispered in his ear, raising goose bumps along his skin. "Especially if someone's been in the house. It's dangerous."

He seriously doubted international spies were a threat to a rodent, but he kept his opinions to himself.

Lucy nuzzled Mr. Nibbles's cheek, and an unexpected twinge of jealousy surprised him. Had that little rat just winked at him? *No.* It must be a trick of the light. No sane person was jealous of a guinea pig. That was ridiculous.

Still, he should have known she'd never have something as common as a cat or a dog as a pet. Her home, much like Lucy herself, was eclectic, warm and mischievous. The mix of colors and patterns was charming. He'd never gone beyond beige in choosing a wall shade, but he didn't mind the startling teal blue Lucy had chosen. Still, had he seen a color swatch, he'd have balked.

Did opposites really attract? Brandt had summed up Jordan's personality as "brunch." He wasn't too early and he wasn't too late—he was someone everyone could agree on. Despite their differences, they'd made a good team. Jordan had tempered Brandt's impulsive tendencies, while Brandt had forced Jordan to take more risks.

Jordan glanced at a watercolor of a woman in a sequined leotard reclining beneath the raised foot of an elephant. The past few months had stripped all the whimsy from his life. His soft edges had been sharpened, and the only humor he had left was dark. Since the bombing, something inside him had changed. There was a restless longing that hadn't been there before.

"Here." Without waiting for an answer, Lucy thrust Mr. Nibbles into his outstretched hands. "Can you hold him for a sec?"

"Wait," Jordan protested. "I don't think this is—"

"I'll be right back." She waved her index finger playfully. "Don't you two get into any trouble while I'm gone."

Leaving Jordan sputtering, she disappeared up the stairs once more.

He stared at the rodent. After a tense moment, Mr. Nibbles blinked.

"Let's get something straight. I'm not a guinea pig person." Jordan assumed his sternest expression—the expression that parted crowds and ensured that his subordinates didn't turn into insubordinates. Right then, he didn't care who was listening. "We're not going to be pals, so don't get any ideas."

The message must have landed, because Mr. Nibbles promptly bit him.

"Ouch." Holding the squirming rodent away from his body, Jordan wrestled open the lid to the cage. "That's no way to make a friend."

Gingerly he replaced the guinea pig and stepped back. Mr. Nibbles scurried to the corner, scuffed in his bedding and promptly began to gnaw on something. Jordan leaned closer.

"No biting," he warned.

Carefully brushing the shaved wood chip bedding aside, Jordan discovered a small, square photograph from an instant camera. As he squinted at the grainy picture, his adrenaline spiked.

He slid his hand into his jacket and closed his fingers around the barrel of his weapon. For a long moment, he stayed very still, his senses attuned to any disturbance. The only sounds were Lucy's footsteps overhead and the gentle scuffing of Mr. Nibbles. The air stirred, and a sheer curtain fluttered in the gentle breeze. He glanced at the photograph once more.

Someone must have slipped it through the open window only moments before. A rare moment of indecision plagued him. Too much time had passed. There was no point in giving chase, and he didn't want to leave Lucy alone.

She returned from upstairs and he pivoted. "We need to go. Quickly."

"Not without Mr. Nibbles."

"Oh, fine," he muttered, returning for the cage. He stared the guinea pig in the eye. "You owe me for coming back for you."

He kept his tone light to avoid further worrying Lucy, then caught himself. If he was distracted by his feelings, he was liable to walk them both right into a trap.

Someone out there was watching them. Waiting for them.

FOUR

A great weight pressed into Lucy's chest, restricting her breathing.

The instant photograph was small, only a few inches square, and the colors were bleached. The two grainy forms in the foreground were barely distinguishable as her and Jordan. Despite the poor quality, there was no mistaking the content. The picture was of the two of them and had been taken outside her sunroom only moments before.

Jordan slammed the trunk and climbed into the driver's seat of Lucy's car. "I checked the angle. It looks like someone took the picture from your neighbor's yard. Are you certain you didn't leave that window open when you left this morning?"

"Positive." She racked her brain for the last time she'd aired that room. "Although it's been a while since I've checked the locks. The sunroom is south facing and heats up quickly in the spring."

Jordan tapped his index finger against the steering wheel. "Whoever planted the listening devices probably left it open as a bit of insurance for easy access to the house when necessary."

"Do you think they know we discovered the surveillance?"

"Even if they did, I don't think they care. They want you to know you're being monitored. Someone took the picture from the neighboring yard, then slipped it through the open window while we were upstairs. They want you to feel on edge. To feel trapped."

Lucy huffed. "It's working."

She'd been vacillating between anger and terror since leaving the house. Content to sit on her lap, Mr. Nibbles gnawed on the edge of the photo until Jordan wrestled it away.

"That's evidence," he admonished lightly. "Stick to your carrots."

He tucked the photo into his breast pocket and ran his fingers through his hair, then twisted around to reach into the back seat. A slight puckering of the skin near his left ear caught her attention. He wore his hair longer than Brandt, and she'd attributed the style to a subtle, maybe even subconscious, bit of rebellion. As she looked closer, she recognized the faint edges of a significant scar.

A chill gripped her. His hair wasn't a fashion statement—it was camouflage.

"We'll wait here a minute," he said. "Westover and Karp are checking the perimeter."

"Okay," she murmured.

They'd told her little about the blast, and she knew only what she'd seen on the news. A suicide bomber had targeted the hotel where Jordan and Brandt had been staying. Two locals had been killed along with Brandt.

Jordan had been outside the building at the time of the attack and was struck by shrapnel. She'd known he was in the hospital at the time of the funeral, but not once had it occurred to her that he might still be in rehab this whole time.

The bombing had happened a year before, and yet he'd only recently made contact. The delay hadn't seemed ominous to her before seeing the signs of his injuries.

Mr. Nibbles squirmed in her hands, nudging her back to the present. "What happens next?"

"We wait. He wants inside your head. He wants you looking over your shoulder. When he figures you're nice and jumpy, he'll make contact."

The black SUV pulled to a stop beside them, and Westover rolled down his window. "There's no sign of anyone. They must have hightailed it out of here after taking the picture. No one went by us, which means they came down the alley. Doesn't look like anyone has a security camera or a doorbell camera pointed in that direction, and the neighboring house is empty and listed for sale. No help there."

"I'd really like to catch a break one of these days," Jordan grumbled. "Where to next?"

Karp passed a piece of paper over Westover and through the open window. "Take Ms. Sutton back to base housing. Westover and I will coordinate with local law enforcement. I don't want to startle whoever did this, but we'll have the police increase the patrols around her house."

Jordan glanced at the paper, and his features relaxed. "Who else are we bringing in on this?"

"If need be, we can coordinate with the local FBI. I'll send any security footage we dig up back to Maryland for analysis. For now, let's figure out what we're dealing with."

"All right."

The window slid back into place and the SUV pulled away.

"I'm sorry," Lucy said, not quite certain what she was apologizing for.

"No need to be sorry. This is what I do." Jordan grunted. "Well, not precisely. Normally I'm running offense. But you're in good hands. I'll coordinate with my staff in Maryland. I trust Karp and he knows the staff here."

"Are you in Omaha for long?" Lucy asked.

She and Brandt had met through mutual friends at a party when he was in town for work. Though Brandt had never been particularly forthcoming about his job, she knew enough about the local base to recognize the communications he monitored were highly classified. Though drones were operated from a separate location, she occasionally visited when the software was updated.

Jordan flashed a wry grin. "My plans are up in the air right now. Had kind of a busy day."

"That's fair." She chuckled in spite of herself. "This isn't how I expected my day to go, either."

"What *did* you have planned?"

"I was going to clean out the refrigerator and weed the garden." This morning seemed like ages ago. She'd have to ask a neighbor to water her flowers if she was gone for long. "Then I was thinking about reading a book and watching some TV. Probably not as exciting as your life, eh?"

A shadow passed over his expression. "Most of my days are the same." His stomach rumbled, filling the silence, and his cheeks flushed. "I was also planning on getting something to eat."

Though she wasn't hungry, Lucy said, "I'm starving."

His obvious relief more than made up for the little white lie. She sensed he'd ignore his own needs in order to take care of hers first.

"How do you feel about burgers?" he asked.

This time she didn't have to lie. "I adore them."

The next instant, she flashed back to the coffee shop. She pictured the shattered windows and heard the noise. Her hand drifted to her bandaged cheek. The weight settled on her chest once more, and she fought the pressure building behind her eyes.

Jordan placed his hand next to hers on the seat, not quite touching. "Don't worry. I know a really good drive-through burger joint. We won't even have to get out of the car."

Grateful for his understanding, she heaved a sigh of relief. "Thank you."

"It gets better, you know. But it takes time. When something like this happens, it changes you. Don't be afraid to talk about it."

Her throat constricted, preventing her from answering, and she nodded instead. Brandt had always assured her that his job was boring and monotonous. He'd downplayed the danger. He'd lied to her. While she recognized that he was trying to protect her, the truth would have served her better. She didn't want to think about what Jordan's life was like when he was in the field.

If this morning was any indication of the kind of danger he faced when he was working overseas, she was better off not knowing the details.

A short time later, the delightful aroma of burgers and fries filled the car. Holding the bag in her lap, Lucy's mouth watered. Maybe she was hungry, after all.

Jordan flashed his credentials to pass through the gate at the air force base and parked her car before a rather dull and sterile-looking building.

Safely sequestered behind a guarded gate, she was struck with an unexpected sense of calm, as though she was leaving the dangerous world behind. Jordan must have felt something similar, because he appeared more relaxed than he had all day.

She carried the food and overnight bag down the hallway while he struggled with the guinea pig cage.

Pausing before a nondescript door, Jordan gestured with his shoulder. "There's an empty apartment down the hall. I'll get your key after we eat. These fries aren't much good if they're cold." Propping the cage on his bent knee to open the door, he met her gaze. "I'm not certain if pets are strictly allowed, so we'll keep this guy under wraps."

"Don't worry. He's very quiet."

The inside of the temporary housing was as bland as the outside. The space reminded her of an extended-stay hotel. There was a small kitchenette and living room along with two closed doors that she presumed led to a bedroom and bathroom.

The moment they sat down, Lucy's appetite returned with a vengeance. In a flurry of paper wrapping and napkins, they devoured their dinner in companionable silence. She glanced at the clock, shocked to see that it was barely six.

"I can't believe it's not midnight," she said. "I feel like it should be dark outside."

Jordan balled his wrapper and stuck it back in the empty sack. "You're telling me."

He stretched his arm and winced, then rubbed his shoulder.

Lucy cleared her throat. "They didn't tell me much about the bombing. Were you...were you hurt badly?"

He shrugged. "Not bad."

She glanced at the table. "I know it's none of my business. I just wondered." She made a vague gesture beside her face. "I saw the scarring earlier. When we were in the car. Was that from...was that from what happened?"

He started to say something, then appeared to change his mind. "Yes." He threaded his fingers through his hair, revealing only a brief hint of the scar before dropping his hand. "I caught some shrapnel from the blast."

"It's okay if you don't want to talk about it."

She didn't know why she needed to know, but being here, after what had happened this morning, she wanted to learn everything about him. She wanted to understand who he was as a person beyond what she'd heard from Brandt.

"It's all right." He stood and crossed to the garbage can. "I don't really remember much about that day. I'd gone to the local market." After pressing his toe against the lever, he tossed in the remainder of their shared dinner. "You'd love the markets there. Everything is colorful and exotic. The sights, the smells, the food. I usually bring something back for my family. My stepsister is expecting. I thought I'd get something for the new baby."

Since he hadn't lingered on the topic, she decided not to press him. "Do you have any other siblings?"

"Nope."

She didn't know why it surprised her to think of him as having a stepsister. He seemed solitary, but that was only because they'd met under such odd circumstances. "Do you get to see your stepsister often?"

His expression grew wistful. "Not as much as I'd like. But I'm trying to be better. After I got out of the hospital, I stayed with my dad for a few weeks in Florida. Then I stayed with my stepsister for a few days. She's only been married a little over a year, and I didn't want to overstay my welcome."

Lucy planted her chin on her hand. "You're fortunate, you know? I always wanted a brother or a sister I was close to. It's lonely growing up as an only child."

"I can relate more than you think. I was twelve when my dad remarried. I was used to being alone. It took me a while to adjust."

"I suppose it would." Her smile was pensive. "But at least you had someone else to blame when there were cookies missing from the cookie jar. I've always wanted to talk with someone else who shared my memories of growing up. It'd be nice to have more family. More company."

"There's that." He returned to his seat across from her. "Emma and her husband visited here once. He's a good guy. We caught a college football game. Now that she's getting closer to having the baby, she doesn't like to travel as much."

Lucy glanced around the room, noticing for

the first time the signs of a prolonged stay. There were even a few framed pictures on a shelf and, alongside, a lonely stack of hardback books.

"How long have you been here?" she asked.

"Almost four months."

She started, surprised and unexpectedly hurt that he'd been this close the whole time and had only just reached out. "I didn't realize."

Then again, she hadn't exactly given him any reason to think she'd welcome a visit. She'd been too wrapped up in herself and her own suffering.

Jordan straightened the salt and pepper shakers on the kitchen table. "We're implementing a new program to monitor overseas communications. We've got at least another six months before rollout. After that, I'm back to Maryland. That's where the National Security Agency headquarters is located. But you already know that."

They'd both had a long and difficult day, and Jordan deserved time to himself, yet Lucy found herself lingering. She'd been grieving by herself for so long, and now she didn't have to be alone.

All of her memories of Brandt came with an ache. Having Jordan here, knowing he understood her loss, she recalled the good times. The happiness and the laughter. The hope. And the ache didn't seem quite as bad as it had before.

"Where does your stepsister live?" she asked.

"Texas." He pointed out a picture of a smiling couple standing before a two-story house with a wraparound porch. "We weren't close growing up, and I regret that. It was a second marriage for both our parents. She'd recently lost her dad and wasn't happy that we'd come into her life. I suppose she felt like my dad was trying to replace the one she'd lost. It's hard for kids." He shook his head. "I'm sorry. I shouldn't be telling you all this."

"No," she protested. "Please. I want to know. It helps. The talking."

An emotion she hadn't felt in a long time stirred inside her. She longed for something more in her life. But if she stepped outside the numbness, she'd have to open herself up to pain. To loss. And she wasn't ready. Not yet.

Jordan made a vague motion toward his bookshelf. "Her name is Emma Lyons—"

"The journalist?"

"Yes."

Lucy gasped and half rose from her chair. "I know her! I know her books. She wrote *Unforgotten*. She wrote that other one." She snapped her fingers, dredging up the memory. "She

wrote the book about *the* Lone Star State Killer.
Which means you're *the* Jordan Harris."

"Yeah," he agreed, clearly bemused. "I'm Jordan Harris."

"The two of you found…" She trailed off. "I'm sorry. Maybe you don't want to talk about it."

"No. It's all right. I'm growing accustomed to the questions." He scratched his temple with his index finger. "You know most of the story if you read the book. When we were kids, the two of us found the body of a woman who'd been murdered. We were on vacation. Camping. Emma became obsessed with serial killers after that. She wrote about them. She studied them. Though she didn't realize it at the time, she even managed to hunt one."

Lucy sat in bemused silence for a few moments. "What a small world."

"Yeah."

The steady hum of the refrigerator filled the silence, and she wished she'd brought her e-reader. She wanted to find Emma Lyons's book again, now that she knew Jordan was featured. She had only a vague memory of a dramatic shoot-out when the killer kidnapped Emma.

Brandt had never mentioned the incident to her, and she wondered if he'd even known about it. Jordan had admitted the connection only when she'd cornered him.

He rubbed a hand over his eyes and stifled a yawn. He was exhausted.

"Well, uh…" She glanced around. "I should be going."

Jordan stood. "I'll get the key. I'll be right back."

When he returned a few moments later, she reached for Mr. Nibbles. "Thank you. For everything. I don't know what I'd have done without you."

He lifted the cage before she could protest. "I'll get that."

She peered inside. "He looks tired."

"He looks ornery."

"That, too. Although looks can be deceiving."

She stepped on her sore ankle and winced. Jordan looped his free hand beneath her arm and steadied her. Her pulse kicked into overdrive. She was confused by the feelings he stirred in her and the spark of awareness at his touch.

Testing her weight once more, she moved away. "It's fine. Just a twinge when I step wrong."

He walked her down the hallway and showed her into a small apartment that was a mirror image of his own, right down to the kitchenette.

As she arranged the cage, he hovered in the doorway. "You've got my number. I'm down the hall if you need anything."

"Thank you." Unsure what the future might hold, she screwed up her courage and said, "I should have written to you or something. I'm sorry. I knew you were hurt. I didn't know… I didn't know if you'd want to hear from me."

His expression was inscrutable. "I wasn't sure of your response, either. I missed your emails, though. When I think of Brandt, I think about him reading your stories. I remember how happy you made him."

Tears pressed against the backs of her eyes. "That's all I ever wanted."

Guilt and sorrow tugged her in opposite directions. Even though the fear was a relief from the oppressive pain, she didn't welcome either emotion. She wanted to retreat into the oblivion she'd grown accustomed to before Jordan's arrival.

"Get some sleep," he said, backing into the corridor. "Chances are, we'll have this whole thing wrapped up by tomorrow and this will all just be a bad memory."

"I hope so."

The door swung closed behind him and she stood unmoving for a long moment. Isolated with her thoughts, she reached for her phone. She wasn't quite ready to be alone. Not yet. Without giving herself time to reconsider, she quickly dialed the number.

After several rings, her mom picked up.

"Is this important, Lucy?" she demanded without preamble. "I was just walking out the door."

Lucy studied the ceiling. "No. It's nothing important."

"Okay, then. Call me back next week. I'm leaving for California tomorrow."

"Oh. Uh, you didn't say anything about taking a trip."

"Didn't I? Well, I'm telling you now." Noises sounded. "I saw on the news there was a shooting in your neighborhood this morning. Really, Lucy, it's time you grew up. You're an adult now. You shouldn't be living in such a…a bohemian…area of town."

"I like my neighborhood."

"That neighborhood is for millennials who claim they want to be artists but are really just living off their parents." She huffed. "Maybe you'd get a promotion at work if you did something about that hair. It's all connected. If you made more money, you could afford something nicer."

"There's nothing wrong with my hair."

"No one will ever take you seriously until you change your style. It was mildly amusing when you were sixteen. People expect a little rebellion out of a teenager. When you're twenty-six, it's embarrassing. Now you're turning into a recluse, as well. When was the last time you left the house?"

"It was a rough year, Mom."

"Not that again. Is this still about that guy you got engaged to after only dating for six months? I read in Dear Amy that you shouldn't mourn a relationship longer than you were in the relationship. And it's been a year. There's no point in wallowing in self-pity. You have a good job, even if you could do better. A good life. Enjoy it."

"I better let you go." Lucy sucked in a jagged breath. "You have a safe trip."

Calling her mom was a mistake. Vicky Sutton wasn't going to change, and it was Lucy's own fault for expecting something different. At least now she didn't have to feel guilty about not mentioning that she was present at the shooting. There was a chance this would all be over by the time her mom got back from California.

"Lucy? Are you still there?"

"Yes."

"We'll talk more next month. My friend Donna has a lovely town house in West Omaha. We'll tour her complex. Just don't wear those awful combat boots."

"Love you, Mom."

"All right, then. We'll talk more about this when I get back."

After disconnecting the phone, Lucy stared at the wall for several long minutes.

A knock sounded, and she opened the door to Jordan.

He smiled sheepishly and extended his arm. "I found some carrots in the fridge for your guinea pig."

Their fingers brushed and her heart did an unexpected little hopscotch. "Thanks. You didn't have to do that."

"I wanted to."

He was gone just that quickly, and she stared at the pile of carrots, absurdly touched by the gesture. He was a good man. He'd been a good and loyal friend to Brandt. Despite the circumstances, she was glad he was here.

Jordan had given her something she hadn't had in a very long time. He'd given her something to look forward to.

He'd given her *someone* to look forward to.

FIVE

Three long days after the shooting at the coffee shop, the tension in the room was palpable. Jordan had assembled his team, and they'd taken over a conference space in a satellite office. The wood-grain-laminate table was littered with coffee cups and notepads.

Jordan turned to Lucy. "Are you certain you haven't been contacted on any additional platforms?"

She was beautiful this morning. Not in the classical sense. Not in the way television and movies wanted to convince people someone was beautiful. There was nothing plastic or made-up about her. Instead, there was just something alluring about her.

He'd spoken with his stepsister, Emma, the previous evening, and he hadn't been able to describe Lucy in a way that did her justice. *She's unique*—that was the best he'd been able to come up with, and that description was woefully inadequate.

"Nothing here," Westover said. "We've got a track on her connections."

The IT department at the National Security Agency had cloned Lucy's phone, and they were monitoring for any contact from the buyer. As the days passed without any news, the team had grown edgy and impatient.

"No one has approached me," Lucy said. She mumbled beneath her breath, "Just like I'm certain Mr. Nibbles doesn't bite."

They'd been having the same lighthearted argument for several days.

"I rescued him from international spies," Jordan whispered. "We're brothers in arms."

"I made you rescue him."

"A minor detail."

Though clearly frustrated by her forced confinement, Lucy was taking her altered circumstances like a champ. A sucker for hardcover books, she'd borrowed a selection from his meager collection. He'd been reluctant to loan her his stepsister's book because Emma had written him in a more heroic light than he deserved, but Lucy had been relentless. They'd also discovered they both had a passion for spy novels. Go figure.

Karp stared at them over his wire-rimmed

glasses. "Would you two like to share with the rest of the class?"

Jordan cleared his throat. "I was reminding Ms. Sutton that the photo found in her house—"

"In Mr. Nibbles's cage," she offered helpfully.

"Discovered in the guinea pig cage." He couldn't bring himself to say "Mr. Nibbles" in front of the other guys, and she was well aware of his reluctance. She'd been trying to trick him into saying the name for the past three days. He was standing firm. "The photo yielded no clues. There were no fingerprints. No useful DNA."

"Who uses a Polaroid camera these days?" Westover asked. "That has to be unusual. Is there any way to trace the film?"

"That film is sold in every Walmart in the nation." Karp rolled his eyes. "Those cameras are a fad for teenagers. I bought one for my daughter at Christmas. Apparently, the kids like the novelty of an actual photo instead of a digital print on their phone. Everything old is new again, I guess."

"Seems like overkill," Westover said. "This guy takes a shot at her, then drops by her house to stick a photo in a rodent cage?"

"Guinea pig," Jordan corrected.

At Lucy's sharp glance, he shrugged. Mr. Nibbles was like a little brother. Jordan might find the little rodent an annoying pest, but no one else got to make fun of him.

"I talked with the profilers in Maryland." Karp typed something on his computer. "They agree with Jordan. The buyer wants her to know who's in control of the situation. She didn't play along the first time, and now he's showing her who has the power."

Westover lifted his head. "You think the buyer is doing his own dirty work? Seems risky."

"Not likely." Karp glanced at Jordan. "What do you think?"

"The shooter is a contract player. He's got to be. He's showing off, but not for us. He's trying to make a name for himself. And I doubt he's working alone. We find him, and we can trace him back to the buyer."

Karp pushed up his glasses and rubbed his eyes. "We're leaving no stone unturned, but we've still got nothing."

A deep wrinkle creased his forehead. He was frustrated. They all were.

They were operating on an unproved theory with dozens of unknowns. Each day without a demand put Lucy at risk. While Jordan was accustomed to honing his patience, this case was different.

His edginess was out of character. He sometimes sat for weeks, even months, waiting for the right opportunity to plant his equipment. And that was only the beginning. When the devices were in place, the true waiting began. He once tracked the occupants of a single residence for three months.

"Why don't we have Lucy reach out?" Westover drummed his fingers on the table. "Get the ball rolling."

Though Jordan had considered the idea already, he hesitated. Lucy's face was grave, and conflicting thoughts swirled through his head. His rusted nerve endings rattled and sputtered. He had an uncharacteristic desire to comfort her, but she needed a protector and a friend. He'd repressed his feelings for a reason, and that reason was still valid. She was off-limits.

She needed to know her safety was his number one priority.

"What's the risk analysis on making contact ourselves?" Karp asked. "We don't know if the impostor has initiated contact again. We could blow this whole thing."

"Let's consider what we know for certain." Jordan retreated to the familiar. There was no use in speculating. "We have evidence that someone is impersonating Lucy in order to steal classified information. Have we learned anything new about the impersonator?"

Karp flipped his laptop screen around.

"While the impersonator made a couple of trial runs, Consolidated Unlimited sent over the security recordings from the night she attempted to access the database."

The black-and-white time-stamped footage showed a woman driving into the parking lot. Her head down, the woman exited her car and used a fob to enter the building. The eerie silence lent the scene an unnerving quality, and the resemblance to Lucy was striking. The hair was a match, and the size and build were similar.

Lucy gasped. "That's not me."

Jordan agreed. Lucy had a unique, purposeful gait paired with an oddly distracted quality. The disguise was superficial at best. The suspect must have known the masquerade wouldn't hold up under close scrutiny. She only needed to fool a night security guard who didn't see Lucy on a regular basis.

Karp collapsed the screen of the playback. "The fob was an unregistered backup kept at the reception desk in case an employee forgot theirs. The receptionist isn't certain when it went missing. The intruder logged in to Vance Eagan's computer at 8:32 p.m. Mr. Eagan kept his password written on the bottom of his keyboard. He no longer does that. The intruder then attempted to access a secure drive. The attempt failed. At 8:55 p.m., she exited the building."

"What about the car she drove?" Westover asked. "Anything traceable?"

"Nothing. The plates were stolen. The make and model were similar to Lucy's. Close enough to access a secure parking lot, anyway. We're checking into police reports and impound lots. Chances are, it's been abandoned by now."

Lucy shivered and rubbed her cheeks. "It's such a weird feeling to see someone who looks like you but isn't you."

"And we're sure it wasn't Ms. Sutton?" Westover rested his elbows on the molded chair arms and tapped his pencil against the table. "Have we checked her alibi?"

Lucy flushed. "I was at the grocery store."

"Receipts and security footage back up her claim," Jordan said, straightening.

If Westover had doubts, he needed to raise them before Lucy was in the room. It was like having a Saint Bernard puppy in a tea shop. Some situations required finesse.

"Got it," Westover said. "Did Consolidated Unlimited identify the targeted files?"

"Yep." Karp almost cracked a smile. "We believe the buyer is after the secure satellite uplink. But the hacker failed to enter the proper code before she was shut out of the system."

"And since the buyer doesn't know he was dealing with a doppelgänger," Jordan added, "he's putting pressure on the *real* Lucy to hand over the information."

Karp took a sip of his coffee. "My guess is that at least one payment has been exchanged, and the buyer wants his money's worth."

"Clever." Westover's pencil stilled. "The impostor left Lucy on the hook and walked away with no one the wiser. Until the shooting, that is."

"That's our working theory," Karp said. "We uncovered the two previous texts sent to Lucy from the buyer. We believe her inaction precipitated the attack at the coffee shop."

"If they wanted my attention, they got it." Lucy stabbed her fingers through her platinum hair, revealing the vivid blue highlights. "But how did they get my phone number in the first place?"

"Anywhere," Jordan said, distracted. He was fascinated by those blue streaks. The way they peeked in and out of her platinum hair was irresistible. "Ten minutes on the internet and I could have the private phone numbers of half the people in this building. And it's probably not the first time this guy has dealt with a reluctant seller. People back out of deals all the time. Sometimes their conscience kicks in. Sometimes it's just fear. Our buyer must have counted on the latter, because he went for the full shock-and-awe campaign."

Seven shots, fifteen seconds apart.

Jordan's stomach plunged. He had no illusions his actions had made any difference that day. The shots were fired with methodical precision, and they'd all been aimed well above Lucy's height. The ploy was deliberate and risky. Whoever wanted the classified information was willing to play fast and loose with Lucy's life.

"So why the sudden radio silence?" Westover asked.

"Something scared him." Jordan sensed they were barreling toward a point of no return, and the muscles along his shoulder blades tightened. "Are we any closer to discovering the buyer's identity?"

He'd cling to the single slender thread of hope that might put an end to all this.

"'Fraid not." Karp clicked through a few more screens. A grainy picture of a dark-haired man in his midthirties appeared. "We're not even sure if this picture is accurate. He's got so many aliases we refer to him only as the buyer. As far as we know, he operates as a middleman. He steals the intel and sells it to the highest bidder. The one IP address the NSA was able to trace puts him local. We believe he illegally acquired the software used to shut down the power grids in three South American nations last year. This is the closest we've ever gotten to the guy, and I want him. I want him bad."

"Can't we narrow down his identity through his customers?" Lucy asked. "Find out who wants a secure uplink to an American drone and go from there?"

"These days, the answer is everyone." Jordan rubbed a weary hand over his eyes. A bombed-out hotel and a flag-draped coffin flashed through his head. "We still have troops on the ground overseas, and American interests are often at odds with foreign investors. A lot of the areas with untapped mineral and oil reserves are still controlled by insurgents. Which is why they're untapped. Few governments are willing to openly challenge the United States and support the insurgents for jurisdiction. If the uplink to the drones is compromised, the bombs miss their targets, or the camera points the other way and the foreign assets are protected. At the risk of American interests." He let the weight of the ramifications settle over the room. "And American lives."

"Then what if he's moved on?" Westover asked. "It's been three days. What if the buyer has given up?"

"Not likely." Karp shuffled through his stack of papers. "We may have scared him, but he'll be back. We need him to believe that Lucy is still interested in making a deal."

Jordan leaned forward and planted his elbows on the table. "Then why don't we send in an agent? A professional. Lucy is a civilian. She doesn't need to be wrapped up in this."

"We can't," Karp said, his expression implacable. "Lucy has to go back to work. Everything should appear normal. This is an inside job. One of her coworkers set her up to take the fall. If they smell a trap, we risk blowing the whole operation."

"Then what next?" Jordan asked, collapsing back in his chair.

"The risk analysis is clear." Karp shut his laptop. "We send a message to the buyer. It's the only way to know for certain."

A cold sweat broke out across Jordan's forehead and neck. Even the idea of dangling Lucy as bait left him feeling as though he was careening out of control. "It's risky. We have to consider Lucy's safety."

"I want to." Lucy spoke up. "We know where the listening devices are located in the house. I can go back home. Give him a show. Make sure he knows I'm still interested in selling the classified information. Maybe I can talk about having money problems or something. I can talk about being in debt."

"How is that safe?" Jordan threw up his hands. "This guy has walked in and out of your house like it has a revolving door."

"That was before I had you guys," Lucy challenged. "Now we have our own surveillance equipment. The house next door is for sale. You guys can set up shop and keep an eye on me from there. That's what they do in the movies, right?"

Westover reached for his notepad. "I'm on it. I'll call the Realtor for the property this evening."

"No." Jordan didn't even realize he'd said the word aloud until everyone turned in his direction. "I'm not certain she fully understands the risk."

"I understand better than anyone," Lucy declared. "The warning at the coffee shop was meant for me. Someone was in my house. Someone has been listening to me for days, maybe even weeks. They took my privacy. They stole my sense of safety when they did that. I might as well lean in."

A silent battle raged between them. She was right, and they both knew it. Anything they did that was out of the ordinary risked tipping off both the buyer and the seller. They were walking a razor-thin line between two competing forces. Without knowing the identities of the two parties involved, they were flying blind.

"We appreciate your dedication, Ms. Sutton." Karp pulled a paper from the stack before him. "Which brings us to our second problem. The impostor—we'll call her the seller. If the seller changes her mind about making the deal, it could blow everything. We have to approach the problem on two fronts. We have to discover the identities of both the buyer *and* the seller."

Jordan raised his arm before Westover had a chance. "I'll go undercover with Consolidated Unlimited."

The other agent glared at him. Jordan suspected he wanted the opportunity to be near Lucy. While Jordan might be guilty of the same desire, at least he knew where to set the boundaries.

"Excellent," Karp said. "But before we waste that effort, is there any chance the employee who made the original deal was scared enough to quit work?"

"Not likely." Westover indicated a list on his notepad. "I spoke with the human resources department at Consolidated Unlimited. No employees have quit recently. No employees have been terminated, either. Not in the past six weeks and that's within our time frame. We believe whoever instigated all this is still working there."

"Good." Jordan's unease was growing despite his outward support of the plan. "We'll start by looking into employees, partners, spouses and relatives. We'll look for anyone with Lucy's size and build. If this was an inside job, then Lucy's impostor has a connection with someone who works in the building."

He hoped his skills hadn't rusted. He hadn't been on a stateside assignment in years. Either way, he wasn't backing down. He'd made a promise to look out for Lucy, and he meant to keep that promise.

Karp threaded his fingers behind his head and leaned back. "Anything else I should know?"

"One other thing," Jordan said quietly. "I'll fill you in privately."

Lucy cast him a sharp glance.

He wasn't ready to tell her about the duplicate ring just yet. There was no reason to conclude that it had anything to do with the current situation. There'd been an inquiry after the bombing, and Jordan had requested a review of the materials. He'd indicated his concern over the purchase. He'd done his due diligence. If something came of it, he'd add the information to what they knew.

Until then, all he had was a ring. It had been lost for nearly a year; another couple of weeks wasn't going to make a difference one way or the other. At least not to Lucy.

She flashed her phone in their direction. "There. I texted. I told the buyer I wanted to meet."

SIX

Jordan's stomach plunged and the room descended into noisy chatter.

Karp held up his hand. "Miss Sutton—"

"You want everything to appear normal." She lifted one shoulder in a careless shrug. "And this is what's normal for me. If someone ghosts me for three days, I'm going to reach out."

"All right. It's done." Karp flashed his palms. "We move forward. But Agent Harris is right. This is an extremely dangerous situation. We need to proceed with caution."

Jordan's phone buzzed. Soon a cacophony of similar notifications ping-ponged across the table. Chairs were shuffled. People reached for the phones.

He glanced at his screen, and his pulse spiked. "I guess that settles it."

"What?" Lucy glanced around the table. "What's happened?"

Any sense of control Jordan might have had evaporated.

"Your message worked," Jordan said grimly. For better or worse, this was out of his hands. "The buyer wants proof that Lucy is still in play."

He searched Lucy's face for any sign of fear or reluctance.

Her expression stoic, she sat back in her seat. "I don't understand. Is he requesting a meeting?"

"Not exactly," he said. "It's what's called a dead drop. You'll leave the information, and we follow the trail."

Jordan sensed she was scared, but there was no way she was going to voice it. Lucy wasn't skilled in deception. Not that he minded. He much preferred to know what she was feeling.

"Two hours," Jordan replied. This was a nightmare scenario. "It's not enough time. We can't scramble a local law enforcement team in two hours. We'll be working with a skeleton crew."

"We only need a skeleton crew," Westover said. "This is a test. If Lucy fails the test, it's back to square one."

"We knew this was a possibility." Karp lifted his phone to his ear. "I can have her wired for video and sound in an hour."

Jordan shook his head. "If the buyer shows up in person for the pickup, we can't apprehend him with such a small crew."

"This guy is too smart to show up himself," Karp said. "He'll send a courier. A low-level delivery boy who doesn't do us any good anyway. We take the opportunity to pass the buyer some intel as a good-faith offer. We don't even have to run surveillance. We prove Lucy can deliver. Then we track him through implanted malware."

"I've got a map of the park where he wants the drop." Using his thumb and forefinger, Westover expanded a picture on his phone. "Two entrances. We only need three teams. One on each exit, and one on Lucy."

"I'm in," Lucy said. "I want to do this. The sooner we get this guy, the sooner things can go back to normal for me."

They didn't have enough time for his peace of mind, but Jordan was waging a losing battle. That didn't mean he was going to stop fighting.

"Then I'm with Lucy," he declared.

There was no way he was sitting in a van while she was forced into a deadly game of cat and mouse with someone who wasn't opposed to using violence to get his point across.

Swallowing hard against his fear, he kept his expression neutral.

He knew better than anyone how much life could change in a single day.

The steady tick-tick-tick of Lucy's analog watch bored into her skull.

She was supposed to wait on a stone stairway in an isolated section of the public park that was surrounded by trees and shrubs. The buyer had promised to provide further instructions from there.

Normally she found the sound of her watch comforting—like a peaceful heartbeat. Not today. Reaching into her pocket, she closed her fingers around the flash drive they'd given her. The decoy was loaded with enough data to pass any initial security scans. By the time the buyer discovered the intel was outdated, implanted malware would reveal his location.

Rain clouds had gathered on the horizon, only partially visible through the canopy of tree limbs overhead. An unexpected cold snap had put a chill in the air, and she'd dressed in a boxy army-green raincoat over black leggings and lace-up black combat boots. She shifted from foot to foot and made an attempt to appear nonchalant.

Leaves rustled, and her pulse jerked. It was dusk, and she'd only seen a handful of people on her way through the park. Normally she didn't frighten easily, but today was not a normal day.

Her retro cat-eyed sunglasses were equipped with a wireless video and voice transmitter. According to the rushed briefing she'd gotten in the van on the way over, the GPS beacon was good anywhere on the planet, but the remote recording and audio needed a dedicated signal, and that range was about a mile—two at the most.

The plan had come together with such rapid precision she'd quickly realized Jordan and his team had been preparing for something like this since the first day she received the message.

A noise whipped her around. A thin teenager on a dirt bike bounced down the shallow stone staircase. As he neared the bottom, she stepped out of the way. He skidded to a halt, his back wheel spinning around, kicking up dirt and pebbles.

"Your friend is at the top," he called, before turning away.

"Wait!" she shouted.

He sketched a wave over his shoulder without turning.

The wind picked up once more, and she studied her surroundings.

After only a brief hesitation, she said, "I'm walking up the stairs."

The team could hear her, but they couldn't speak to her. They'd decided an earpiece was too risky in case she was searched.

To calm her frayed nerves, she concentrated on putting one foot in front of the other. A soft mist from the dense rain clouds had turned the stones slick. If she recalled her local lore correctly, this was called the Morphing Stairs because no one was able to count the same number of risers twice.

Her foot slipped and she gasped, catching herself at the last minute. No wonder no one could count them—in some places the stones were little more than piles of pebbles eroded over the years.

Upon reaching the top, she paused to catch her breath. She was in better shape than this, but tension constricted her lungs.

She spun in a circle, searching for her "friend." Had she misunderstood the message?

A lone woman walked her yellow Lab dog in the distance. There was no sign of Jordan and Westover, and she forced herself to breathe. She wasn't supposed to see them. That was the whole point.

The dark-haired middle-aged woman with the yellow Lab caught sight of Lucy and turned in her direction. Lucy glanced over her shoulder before crossing the clearing. Something in the woman's posture indicated she was walking this way with a purpose.

The woman wrestled her dog in the new direction. "Your boyfriend is worried sick about you," she called across the distance. "He's at the top of the hill. Follow the road and you'll probably run into him."

"Are you sure he was looking for me?"

The woman's smile faltered. "Unless there's another woman with platinum hair and an army-green jacket."

Lucy's teeth clattered together. They knew what she was wearing. They'd already seen her.

Someone was probably watching her now. She sucked in a deep breath. Jordan had warned her that something like this might happen. The buyer was likely to make her travel to another location in the park to ensure she hadn't been followed.

"Thanks," she offered with a wan smile. "It's like a maze in here."

The dark-haired woman chuckled. "Yes. You're better off sticking to the path this time of year."

The wind lashed Lucy's hair across her face, and she scraped the strands aside. Nearing the road meant cars. Though everyone had agreed the possibility was unlikely, Jordan had warned her about entering a vehicle.

DO NOT let them take you to a second location.

As a compromise, she kept to the grass. Her boots sank into the loamy earth, leaving deep impressions. Her ankle had healed almost entirely, and there was only a twinge now and again when she stepped the wrong way.

She trudged the length of a football field without encountering her "boyfriend." Once again, she paused to catch her breath.

There were no additional messengers in sight. Either she continued forward or she retraced her steps. Since the buyer was clearly leading her in one direction, she continued following the bend in the road.

As she rounded the corner, she spotted a single car parked before a picnic table pavilion. A familiar figure sat on a bench facing the opposite direction.

Jordan. Even with his back to her, she recognized his posture and picked up her pace. If he was revealing himself, that could only mean one thing. Mission aborted. Had they scared the buyer? Or had this whole thing been an exercise in futility from the beginning?

She hadn't realized how tense she'd been until the fear drained from her muscles. Everything had happened so fast there'd been no opportunity to prepare herself. Next time she'd be ready.

Then again, if they were fortunate, there might never be a next time.

Feeling almost buoyant, she didn't hear the van until it pulled to a stop beside her. A door slammed and a man wearing a ski mask and a leather jacket circled around the front. Her heart raced and she lunged away.

The man snatched Lucy's arm, halting her startled retreat.

"Get in."

She frantically shook her head. "No. That's not the deal. I'm not going."

"This can go easy or go hard," he rasped. "Your choice."

His fingers bit painfully into her arm, and he dragged her toward the back of the van.

She panicked. "Jordan!"

The man gave her a painful shake. "Who's that?"

"My boyfriend," she lied. "You didn't think I'd come to this park alone? At dusk. I'm not stupid."

"You must be." Easily holding her squirming body away from him, he yanked open the rear door of the windowless van. "Because that was real stupid, lady."

The next instant his hold went slack, and he stumbled backward.

Jordan appeared behind him, his fisted hand raised. "Is this guy bothering you?"

"Yes," she shouted, rushing toward him.

Her abductor stumbled upright. His mask had come loose during the scuffle, revealing half of his face and a distinctive collar tattoo. He caught the hood of her coat, yanking her backward. Lucy shrieked and clawed at her neck.

A dark form moved behind Jordan.

"Look out!" she sputtered, her throat constricted by the tight hold on her hood.

To her horror, Jordan crumpled forward, landing in an ungainful heap on the dewy grass.

The second man pulled a gun from his waistband.

"No!" Lucy shouted, clawing at her abductor's arm.

He spun her around to face him and she gasped. His eyes were black, fathomless holes behind his mask. He yanked her closer.

"Dead bodies attract attention," he said, his breath hot against her forehead. "We'll dump him off-site."

Her whole body trembled. The two men hoisted Jordan into the back of the van. This time Lucy didn't struggle when her abductor hauled her to her feet. She had to stay calm. She had to think. She couldn't afford to lose her cool now. There were two more teams watching the exits. They'd come for them. Right?

As she frantically considered her options, a dark cloth dropped over her head, plunging her into darkness.

SEVEN

Jordan's head throbbed.

He was on a boat. It must be a boat because of the gentle rocking. Despite the pain radiating through his skull, his head was cradled on something soft. He moved his fingers, but his wrists were tied before him.

His training kicked in by rote. They must not see him as much of a threat or they'd have secured his hands *behind* his back. He kicked his legs, but his ankles were secured, as well.

He cracked open his eyes to inky blackness.

Lucy.

He moved his head, and a blinding pain sent him gasping.

"It's all right," Lucy said, her voice gentle. "Try not to move. They've locked us in the van."

Jordan's senses gradually came awake through the fog of pain. They were in a moving vehicle, which explained the rocking, and Lucy had cradled his head in her lap. Beneath the scent of exhaust fumes, he caught a hint of her jasmine perfume.

"Are you all right?" he demanded, surging upright. The instant before he was struck on the back of the head came rushing back. When they'd grabbed Lucy, he'd seen red. The rest of his actions had been fueled by a blind rage. "Are you hurt?"

"I'm fine. I'm more worried about you. You probably have a concussion or internal bleeding or something."

"I'm fine. I promise. I've taken worse hits than that over the years." He moved his head and winced. "How long have we been driving?"

"Ten minutes." Her voice caught. "I was afraid they'd killed you."

"Not with this hard head." There were no windows in the service van and the pitch darkness was disconcerting. He had no sense of time or place beyond the moments before he'd been knocked unconscious. "Anything else happen while I was out?"

"They took our phones and I lost my sunglasses during the scuffle." There was a long pause. "They have your gun."

Jordan made a sound of frustration. At least he hadn't been carrying his credentials. Since Lucy had claimed he was her boyfriend, there was no reason for the men to assume otherwise.

As long as the men holding them didn't know she was working with the authorities, they had a chance of getting out of this alive.

"Okay," he said, keeping his voice level. "Did they say anything else?"

"They're not going to kill you." she said. "They talked about pouring whiskey over you and dumping you someplace. I guess they figured if you looked like a drunk, no one would believe you'd been kidnapped. They took the flash drive. I don't know why they've still got us."

Neither did Jordan, and that had him worried. "I messed up their strategy, and they don't know what to do. They don't have a contingency plan."

"I'm sorry." A sob accompanied her words. "I shouldn't have gone near the road. You warned me about getting into a vehicle."

Her fear sliced through him like a knife, and he shook off the unfamiliar emotions crowding him. He reached awkwardly for her bound fingers and threaded their fingers together. Where was their backup? Why hadn't Karp or Westover stopped the van by now?

"It's not your fault. They didn't give you much choice." Jordan twisted his hands, but the zip ties held strong. "You did the right thing. They didn't gag us. Our hands are tied in front of us, which means they aren't very worried about us escaping. They've already said they don't want to kill us. That's all good news."

"It doesn't feel like good news."

Jordan chuckled humorlessly. "One of the NSA teams is tailing us by now. We have to trust they have a plan." The surveillance teams should have spotted them leaving the park. Even if no one had witnessed the kidnapping, a white cargo van was a huge red flag. Except too much time had passed for his peace of mind. "The team will have a BOLO out. That's a 'be on the lookout.' It's only a matter of time before they come for us. Until then, we stick with our story if these guys ask any questions. You're selling classified information, and I'm your overprotective boyfriend."

Her grip on his hand loosened, and he touched her wrist. Her pulse had slowed in the past few minutes, and relief washed through him. Risking her life further was not an option. Whatever happened, he'd see that she came out of this safe and alive.

"What do you think they're going to do with us?" she whispered.

Jordan bent his knees and braced his back against the side of the van, then shifted his body, giving Lucy something softer to lean on than the metal siding. "I don't know. We're on the interstate. They're not going through the city. They certainly don't care if we're screaming our heads off back here or they'd have gagged us." His eyes had adjusted to see vague shapes, and he reached for her hands again. "We'll be fine. Don't worry."

Even without the luxury of sight, the vibrations from the wheels indicated they were going too fast for any kind of an escape attempt. This wasn't like the movies. If they flung themselves out of a moving vehicle at high speeds, they'd be killed.

He felt her move against his shoulder. "You don't have to lie to me. I'd rather know the truth."

"How could you tell I was lying?" He caught her familiar jasmine scent along with citrusy undertones, and his heart rate quickened. "I thought I was doing an excellent job of being reassuring."

"Instinct, I guess. I'd rather you were honest with me."

The van hit a bump, throwing Lucy against him. He shifted, tucking her against his shoulder.

"It's like I said—they're off script." Jordan sighed. She was far too perceptive for her own good. Lying was only going to make things worse, so he might as well be truthful. "They should have left us in the park once I interrupted. They didn't. Now they don't know what to do. Panic leads to bad decision making. That's the part that concerns me."

"Then what do we do? Can you get free?" She released his fingers. "I saw a YouTube video on escaping from zip ties."

She must have twisted her wrists because she inadvertently elbowed him in the ribs.

He grunted. "It won't work."

"Are you certain?" She huffed. "Ouch."

Clumsily he grasped her forearm. "Don't hurt yourself. These guys saw the same video, because they used heavy-duty zip ties. We're not going to break them." He took a deep breath and braced for her reaction to his next words. "They can't afford to let anything happen to you, but I'm expendable. If you see a chance to escape, take it. If I tell you to run, then promise me you'll run and don't look back."

"But—"

"I can take care of myself." He steeled his resolve. "If I'm not worried about you, I'll have a better chance of saving myself."

Another lie. He was going to be worried about Lucy until they had the buyer, the impostor and their abductors in custody. His duty was no longer to his team, but it was to Lucy's safety.

Though he strained his ears, there was nothing to hear beyond the steady whir of the tires against the pavement. "I'm going to see if there's anything in here we can use as a weapon."

Inching along with his bound hands and feet, Jordan traced the rear panel doors and ensured they were locked inside. The rest of his efforts were wasted. The inside of the van was completely and totally empty.

A banging sounded from the front, and Lucy gave a startled yelp. Jordan scooted toward the cab and pressed his ear against the metal partition. The men's voices were muffled but clearly raised in anger. They were arguing, and if he was careful, he could use their discord to his favor.

A slender thread of hope formed within him, and he returned to his seat by Lucy. "How are you holding up?"

She nestled against his side. "I'm scared."

He couldn't think as clearly when she touched him, but she was frightened. If sitting near him made her feel safer, there was no harm in that.

"I'm scared, too," he admitted. "Believe me, I will do everything in my power to get you through this."

"I know you will."

His throat ached with an emotion he was afraid to identify. Everything about this was wrong. He'd promised Brandt he'd look out for

Lucy if anything ever happened to him. Instead, he was risking her life.

Lucy shifted, and the soft silk of her hair brushed the sensitive skin of his neck.

"Why were you sitting at the picnic table?" she asked. "I thought you were supposed to be out of sight. I thought maybe the drop had been called off."

"I would have looked out of place loitering by the stairs. Once you were on the move, it wasn't such a big deal to be seen."

"I'm glad you're here and not Westover. I know it may sound strange, but because you were such a good friend to Brandt, I feel like you're my friend, too, even though we never met before this week. Does that make any sense?"

Guilt coursed through his veins. "I know how you feel." To distract her from their circumstances, he added, "Do you remember that time you dipped your necklace in the ranch dressing?"

He didn't know how far the men planned on taking them, and there wasn't anything to do other than wait until the van slowed. He might as well distract Lucy and talking filled the time.

"How could I forget?" She chuckled. "I leaned over the vegetable tray at the Christmas party and dragged the beaded fringe of my necklace through the dip. By the time I realized what I'd done, I was a mess. I spent the rest of the night with wet blotches on my dress. I figured that might give you guys a laugh."

Most people cultivated a better version of themselves online—a fake, plastic version with a perfect background. Not Lucy. She was open and completely authentic. Although, come to think of it, he didn't recall her telling many stories about her successes. She mostly focused on the silly, clumsy things that happened to her.

Recalling the papers on her desk, he asked, "How did you become a software engineer?"

"Programming is creative, if you think about it. Everything I do is ultimately creative problem-solving."

"I never thought of it that way."

"And also because my mom wanted me to be a doctor." She laughed, though he sensed the emotion was forced. "Computer programming was the furthest I could get from health care."

Her voice was stronger, and her breathing had slowed. Since the diversion was working, he plunged ahead. "Then you've always liked computers?"

"Pretty much. I took a programming class in junior high. The school website was atrocious. I overhauled the whole thing. I even designed a program to send reminders to parents for upcoming sports events. The teacher was so impressed he nominated me for a scholarship my senior year. While I was in college, someone hacked my Facebook account. That was a catalyst, I guess. I became fascinated with cybersecurity. God was looking out for me, because my college was designated a National Center of Academic Excellence in Cyber Operations by the National Security Agency."

"That's a mouthful."

"That just means it was a good place to be if you were fascinated by cybersecurity. Firms that deal in classified material do a lot of recruiting out of the senior class. I took a job at Consolidated Unlimited before I'd even graduated. The rest, as they say, is history."

"And you like what you do?"

"I love it. I can't imagine doing anything else. Most people think what I do is boring, but I find it fascinating. There's always a challenge. I'd like to work in a building with more windows, and sometimes it's frustrating because people don't understand why I can't talk about my work. Other than that, it's great."

"I know what you mean. It's hard to keep secrets from the people you love."

His friends mostly understood what he did for a living and the restrictions on his time, but he hadn't realized what a toll his job was taking on the rest of his family until Emma's accident. His stepsister had assumed his work was more important than her. Nothing was further from the truth. Since then, he'd tried to do a better job of keeping in touch. Especially since she'd gotten married the previous year and was expecting his niece or nephew.

"How about you?" Lucy asked. "How did you end up being a spy?"

"That term is too grandiose for what I do. My mom was the real spy in the family. She worked for the CIA."

"No way!"

"Yep. True story. She did a semester in Germany in college and met my dad there. He was in army telecommunications and stationed in Berlin. They lived in Germany for almost ten years. Here's a piece of trivia for you. I was even born in Berlin."

The sound of the wheels changed with a shift in the pavement, and Jordan noted the difference.

"A Berlin baby," Lucy said. "Wow. I never would have guessed. Now I want to know everything. Did your mom join the CIA in Germany? Or before that? If you tell me, will you have to kill me?"

The oddity of the conversation wasn't lost on him. They might as well be sitting in a coffee shop rather than trapped as hostage victims in the back of the van. Still, as long as Lucy wasn't concentrating on her fear, he was willing to talk.

"They recruited my mom in Germany," he said. "That's about all I know. She was never very forthcoming about the rest of the story. I'm not even certain what she did for them while we lived there. We moved back when I was seven. So there you have it. I was a military brat who spent the first years of my life in another country. America was quite a shock."

"I can't even imagine. Do you speak German?"

"Some. I used to practice with my mom. She was fluent in French, Spanish and German. Dad and I mostly stuck to English." He hadn't thought about Germany in a long while. His time there had been invaluable. He'd learned what it was like to be a foreigner, and the experience had given him a sense of empathy that carried through to his current job. "My parents got divorced when I was a kid. My dad was ready to live in the States. My mom wasn't."

"That must have been hard."

"Honestly, not at first. I was so excited to be in the United States permanently, I couldn't think of much else for a long time. When I got older, I realized how much that must have hurt her. But living stateside was like a dream come true. The American kids on the base in Berlin cycled in and out, and sometimes I went to school with the diplomats' kids, but we only visited the States once or twice a year. While I like being overseas, I like coming home more."

"Is your mom still in the CIA?"

"She passed away a few years ago." The pain was still there, but not as sharp as it had been in the beginning. "Blood clot."

"I'm so sorry."

"She was a tough lady. I never thought anything could kill her." He shook his head, realizing he'd been dominating the conversation when he was supposed to be keeping Lucy's mind off their predicament. "Anyway, that's how I got involved with the Special Collection Service branch of the National Security Agency. It's actually a joint venture with the CIA. I usually just say I work for the Department of Defense because most people have heard of the DOD. My mom had connections, and I had a knack for getting in and out of places without being noticed."

He didn't recall ever telling someone that much about his life and his work. Not even Brandt. Usually, when people asked him questions, he'd offer vague answers and change the subject. Not that he wasn't proud of his life and his parents, but he wasn't generally comfortable talking about himself. There was something about not being able to see Lucy that made it easier to open up to her. Then again, maybe his ease in talking about his life came from Lucy and not just the darkness. She made it easy to talk.

She shifted, and he knew she must be getting uncomfortable. His feet and hands were starting to tingle.

"Do you get to see your dad very often?" she asked.

"Not as much as I should, although I've been trying to be better. These past few months have made that harder."

He hadn't told his dad or Emma the full extent of his injuries, although he was certain his stepsister suspected he was keeping something from them. Emma was still skittish around him, and he regretted the distance. He didn't know how to reassure her that their relationship wasn't going to collapse at the first sign of discord. She didn't trust his loyalty yet, and that hurt.

Lucy lifted her arms and lightly touched the side of his head. "You didn't want anyone to know, did you? You didn't want them to know how badly you were hurt."

The shift in her position brought her face closer, and his lips brushed against her cheek. Everything about this was wrong. They were in grave danger. Lucy was off-limits. Yet for a split second, there was just the two of them. For a moment he let himself imagine this was a cozy booth in an exclusive restaurant. He imagined everything was all right in the world. There were no shadows in the past, no sorrow, no danger. The next instant, reality crashed in.

The vehicle slowed and Jordan tensed, jerking away. "Remember. Whatever happens. Look out for yourself."

Everything in his life, all of his conditioning, all of his training, had led up to this point. Lucy was depending on him.

He had one chance to get this right.

Lucy sucked in a sharp breath.

The van pulled to a stop, though the engine remained running. Doors slammed. The back hatch flew open. Temporarily blinded, she felt more than saw as Jordan was yanked unceremoniously from the vehicle. He stumbled, his balance compromised by his bound hands and feet. They dragged him a few feet before dropping him to the ground.

"The girl, too?" the first man called.

"The girl, too."

Lucy caught the barest hint of her surroundings before one of the men kicked Jordan in the stomach.

She shouted, but the man holding her covered her mouth, preventing her from protesting.

The second man grasped the back of Jordan's neck and pressed his cheek into the neatly manicured grass. "I have your wallet. I have your address. You say anything to the police, anything at all, and I come and find you. You got that? Because if I have to come looking for you, I'm not going to be happy."

"I got it," Jordan replied hoarsely.

The man kicked him again. Lucy's chest ached and her vision blurred.

Doors slammed and the sound of wheels on concrete receded into the distance.

Lucy dropped to the ground, her bound legs curled to the side, her wrists in her lap. Her hair was a wild, tangled mess, and she shook it out of her eyes. Planting his elbow in the grass, Jordan pushed himself to a seated position.

She glanced around, and a dawning sense of horror nearly overcame her. "Do you realize where they've left us?"

"Judging by all the grave markers, I'm guessing this is a cemetery."

Being in a cemetery at dusk wasn't her first choice for a Friday evening excursion. On any other day she might attempt a brave face, but after everything she'd been through this week, she was all out of brave faces.

Jordan studied their surroundings. "Do you know where we are? I'm not familiar with this part of town."

Lush green hills dotted with oak trees undulated toward the horizon. Raised grave markers were scattered among the flat tombstones. A meandering road wove its way through the bucolic scene.

"It's Forest Lawn cemetery," Lucy said. "I've only been here a few times. For funerals. But you probably guessed that. This place is enormous." Tilting back her head, she studied the overcast sky. "They must have driven us around for a while, because we're only five or six miles from where we started."

Though their abductors had treated her far more gently than they'd treated Jordan, her ankles and wrists chafed.

The faint hum of a car engine caught her attention, and her heart raced. "They're coming back!"

EIGHT

Lucy frantically searched for a place to hide. She wasn't going back in the van.

"They won't come back for us, and that's not them," Jordan replied, searching the distance. "I can tell by the engine. It's definitely not the van they were driving."

"How can you tell what kind of engine it is by the sound?" An ancient sedan appeared along the winding road, and her limbs turned to jelly. "You know what? Never mind—I'll take your word for it."

"We'll try and get this driver's attention, but we don't want to scare him. Just follow my lead like you did at the house. You're a natural at this."

Of all the talents God might have bestowed on her, she'd hoped for something a little more righteous than lying on command. In an attempt to act naturally, she sat up straighter and smoothed her hair with her bound wrists. Jordan did the same. Nothing unusual about a couple of folks tied up on the side of the road. Nothing at all.

The car pulled to a stop beside them, and the window was cranked down in a leisurely fashion.

An elderly man in a powder blue suit leaned his gaunt face through the opening. "You folks all right?"

"Yes, sir," Jordan answered with a wide grin. "My friend and I are part of a scavenger hunt. Do you have a knife or a pair of scissors or something to cut these ties?"

"And someone just left you here like this?" The wrinkles in the man's forehead deepened. "Don't seem like much of a game to me."

"Wouldn't be fun if it was easy." Jordan chuckled. "The first team to discover all the clues and return to the starting point wins a hundred dollars."

"I think I'd stay home for that amount of money." The man appeared to consider them for a moment. "I might have a pair of wire cutters in the trunk. That should do the trick."

Lucy and Jordan exchanged a glance. The driver's-side door creaked open and the man swung his legs around. Bracing his hand on the seat, he pushed off into a mostly standing position since his back didn't quite straighten. Jordan kept his goofy grin in place, and Lucy tried to appear as small and harmless as possible.

Jordan cleared his throat. "Rainy weather we're having. Keeping everything nice and green for this time of year."

"That it is. That it is." The man shuffled to the back of his car and popped the trunk. "Don't want too much rain, though. Bad for planting."

"You ever do any farming?"

"Back in the day. My folks had a farm in Elgin. We lease the land now. Everything is big business these days."

Lucy squirmed. Though she didn't want to rush the man, her fingers were going numb and her ankles throbbed. She'd prefer a little less idle chitchat and a little more action.

Jordan tossed her a beseeching glance. "Looks like we're going to get some more rain before this day is over."

"True, true." The trunk slammed. "We're in for another storm tonight. Might have some flooding up north if this keeps up."

The two might have been chatting over breakfast at the local café. If Lucy didn't know better, she'd have fallen for Jordan's story hook, line and sinker. He wasn't flashy like Brandt, but he was steady. There was a calm, consistent quality about him that put everyone around him at ease. Brandt had trusted him implicitly, and now she saw why.

Whether it was giving her a handful of carrots for her guinea pig after a long day or the way he'd held her hand when she was frightened, there was a deep sense of empathy in the tiny kindnesses he performed naturally. While Brandt had favored grand, vivid gestures, Jordan was far subtler. If Brandt was a Rembrandt then Jordan was a Monet—all blurred edges and muted tones, but no less beautiful.

They were opposites, but at the core they were similar. She had no doubt that both men loved deeply and completely. They were both loyal, and both men of faith. Brandt had mentioned as much when they were assigned together.

After what seemed like an eternity, the older man circled around the car carrying a folded Buck knife. He glanced at them and hesitated.

"I'm Jordan and this is Lucy, by the way." Jordan introduced the two of them. "She's from Omaha, but I'm a transplant."

The personal details seemed to put the elderly gentleman more at ease, and her admiration for Jordan grew. They didn't have a lot of other options. If their Good Samaritan balked at setting them free, they risked being here after dark, and Lucy didn't relish the prospect.

No other cars had passed since they'd been there, and the sun was dipping lower on the horizon. The gathering storm clouds had turned the sky unnaturally dark. Lucy shivered.

"My name is Hank." The man shuffled closer. "Whereabouts do you hail from originally if you're a transplant?"

"Maryland," Jordan said. "Most recently from Frederick."

"What brings you to these parts?"

"Work."

"What kind of work?"

"Government work."

Hank carefully unfolded the knife. "Nice to see young people playing games that take them outside. Everyone is always staring at their phones these days. Still, I'm not sure if a cemetery is the most respectable place for this sort of thing. Not sure at all."

Lucy drew her arms together to warm them. Chill moisture from the damp grass had seeped through her layers of clothing. She was miserably cold and bruised from their ordeal.

"Point taken," Jordan readily agreed. "We're really sorry to disturb your evening. You don't happen to have a cell phone, do you?"

"I do have a cell phone," Hank replied. "The grandkids bought me one for my last birthday."

Lucy nearly wept with relief. She was tired and

sore and frightened. The sooner someone from Jordan's team came to rescue them, the better.

Jordan grinned. "You think my girlfriend and I could make a call? We need to figure out our next clue. For the scavenger hunt," he added hastily.

"I'd let you make a call, all right. But it's at home."

Lucy's hand shook as she pressed her fingers against her lips and took a few deep, calming breaths. There was no need to be upset. The lack of a phone was only a minor setback. They were safe, for the moment. They weren't in the back of the van. People were looking for them. There was no need to panic.

Hank scuffled toward Jordan. "Don't know why anyone would need to make a call when they're away from home. What's the point of leaving the house if folks can still find you?" He wrestled open the folded blade. "Why don't I get you taken care of first, young man, and then you can help the little lady."

"Sure thing." Jordan shot her a sympathetic glance. "The sooner we get started, the sooner we'll be finished."

Hank sawed through the zip ties binding Jordan's wrists for what seemed like an eternity. The moment he was free, Jordan took the knife and released his feet, then turned toward Lucy.

He easily sliced through the thick plastic, and she shook out her hands to stop the tingling.

"You folks better hurry up with whatever you're doing," Hank declared. "I was just visiting my wife. She's over in the tranquil gardens. There's a big tree and a park bench where I can sit in the shade and have a chat with her. But the cemetery closes at dusk."

Jordan folded the knife and extended his hand. "We won't keep you. No one wants to be trapped in a cemetery after dark."

Lucy snorted. Least of all her. This place was huge, and she had no idea how far they were from the exit. A neighborhood abutted one side of the Forest Lawn, but as far as she knew, the rest of the area surrounding the cemetery was rural.

"No worries. No worries." Hank tucked the knife into the pocket of his suit.

Lucy sat up straighter. The blood was slowly returning to her legs, and she massaged her calves. Stinging pricks shot up and down her shins, and she didn't trust herself to stand just yet.

Hank squinted. "Is there anything else you two need?"

"Nothing at all." Jordan stood and reached for Lucy. "You've been really helpful."

She clasped his hand and lurched upright. He tucked her against his side to keep her steady.

"You're most welcome," Hank said. "I hope you two have fun on this scavenger hunt of yours."

"I'm sure we will."

The elderly man opened the driver's door. "Seems odd, leaving you all alone in here without a car or anything."

"Don't worry. Our friends will be here soon. We'll be out of here by dusk."

"Alrighty, then."

As he pulled away, Hank stuck his arm out the window in a friendly wave.

"What a sweet man," Lucy said. "I hate to deceive him."

"It's better this way," Jordan said, wearily resigned. "There's really nothing he can do for us without a cell phone, and I don't want to put him in any danger."

Her teeth chattered and she rubbed her upper arms. "What now?"

"We follow the signs to the exit. Let's avoid any local shortcuts. We need to find people. We don't want to avoid them. Worse comes to worst, we can trigger the security alarm—"

The faint sounds of a ringtone interrupted his words.

Lucy cocked her head. "Did you hear that?"

Jordan's eyes widened. "That's my phone."

Energized by the possibility of finding his cell phone, frantically they traced the sound to a section of grass by the side of the road. They discovered Jordan's cell phone, undamaged, near a flat grave marker.

Her own phone hadn't been as fortunate. Lucy sighed. It must have ricocheted off the stone, because the face was smashed.

Jordan glanced at the number and blanched. "I need to take this real quick."

Lucy shrugged. "Sure. Hot date?"

"Not likely."

She was unaccountably relieved; nevertheless, her curiosity was piqued.

Jordan swiped across the screen to accept the call. "Hey, Dad. What's up?… I'm still in Omaha, remember?" He grimaced. "The Global Strike Command is subordinated here, that's why… Yes, it is a cool name… Yes, it's much safer than where I was before… No, I'm not going back overseas anytime soon… How's Emma?… No. I'm not changing the subject."

Lucy gaped. Listening to Jordan speak with his dad was like running into a teacher in the supermarket. While she knew he had a life outside of his NSA work, this was the first time she'd seen evidence of it.

He caught her curious stare and rolled his eyes. Lucy moved a few feet away to give him some privacy, but he motioned with one hand, urging her to stay near. She shifted from foot to foot, concentrating on a tree in the distance.

"Yes. I'm still coming home for Memorial Day... Look, I'm with a friend. Do you mind if I call you back tomorrow?... Yes. It's a girl... No. She's, um, she's a colleague. We're working on a case... I don't always work... I told you, I'm in Omaha, Nebraska. It's probably the safest place on the planet."

Lucy raised her eyebrows and Jordan shrugged.

"All right... I'll see about getting you some steaks. Tell Emma not to worry, either... Yes... Yes... Okay... I will... I love you, too. Bye." Jordan disconnected the call and his cheeks flamed. "Sorry about that. He worries if he can't get ahold of me."

"Don't apologize." Lucy bit the inside of her cheek to keep from smiling. "We owe him. If he hadn't called, we never would have found your phone. Although it's probably for the best that you didn't tell him you were just kidnapped and are stranded in a cemetery."

"Didn't seem like a good idea." Jordan initiated another call. "I'll just see what happened to the team."

"You're fortunate, you know."

He held the phone away from his ear. "How so?"

"It's nice that he worries about you."

Her own mom called on the first Sunday

of each month at precisely five o'clock. Lucy couldn't imagine her mom calling out of the blue just to check on her.

Jordan spoke a few clipped sentences, then listened for several beats before stowing his phone once more. "They're on the way. There was another entrance road into the park that's not marked on the map because it's no longer in use. It didn't show up on the satellite photo because of the vegetation. It's supposed to be blocked, but tire tracks indicate it's been used recently. By the time they realized there was a problem, we were gone. I'm sorry."

"There's nothing to apologize for. I'm the one who insisted on meeting. You were the one with the doubts. If we'd had more time for research, we'd have known about the road."

Judging by his expression, her reassurance didn't make him feel any better. Her heart went out to him. From the very beginning, he'd always kept her safety at the forefront.

He walked a few paces and pivoted on his heel. "The team is about twenty minutes away. Why don't we find a bench or something and sit down? Looks like we might get some rain."

A rumble sounded and she glanced at the sky. A fat raindrop splashed against her arm. Then another. She didn't want to sit down. She didn't know exactly what she wanted. A strange sense of restless energy gripped her. The day of the coffee shop shooting, she'd been exhausted. This time, the fear had energized her. Several more raindrops splashed against her face and arms.

Jordan snatched her hand. "C'mon. This way."

They dashed across the grass toward a petite mausoleum and huddled beneath the narrow overhang. Lucy wrapped her arms around her body. In an instant, the sky seemed to open up and rain poured over them, dripping from their inadequate shelter.

Jordan angled his body and she scooted nearer. His eyes connected with hers, but this time it felt different. This time *she* felt something different. Like a magnet, there was an irresistible pull toward him. She hadn't looked at a man with other than brotherly affection in a long while, and the sensation was heady. She waited for the guilt but found only a deep sense of longing.

"Cold?" he asked.

She nodded.

He reached for her and tugged her close. Her hair slid across his coat as she dropped her head against his shoulder. His warmth immediately enveloped her. She snuggled into his arms, and all she could think of was how good it felt, how right.

"I'll always look out for you," he said, his

arms tightening around her. "And not just because I promised Brandt."

She fisted her hands into the material of his shirt. "You make me feel safe, Jordan."

"We're friends, I hope."

"Yes. I thought I knew you before, even though Brandt did a terrible job of describing you."

A low chuckle vibrated in his chest near her ear.

"I hope the reality is better."

"It is."

"Same here."

It should be easy to think of Jordan as only a friend, but with his arm wrapped around her shoulder, and his scent and heat surrounding her, her thoughts veered into dangerous territory. The wind picked up, pelting them with chilly raindrops.

Jordan reached into his pocket. "I'll call 911. What's the point of avoiding police involvement if we freeze to death? There might be a black-and-white that's closer."

Lucy placed her hand over his. "It's all right. I don't mind the rain."

"Are you sure?"

"We're safe," she said. "We're relatively dry. As long as you don't think they'll come back, we might as well wait."

"They can't afford to come back. We have a

phone. They won't risk it. Did you get a good look at either of them?"

They were cocooned together in relative safety, and the outside world and all its dangers were faraway. Once the rest of the team got here, she'd have to face reality.

Lucy searched her memory for the details of the kidnapping. "One of them had a distinct tattoo on his neck. His mask slipped off during the scuffle. I might be able to sketch it."

"You said you'd been to this cemetery before—"

A thunderous bang reverberated through the valley, the sound carrying over the rain. It was followed in rapid succession by a second loud pop.

Lucy gasped and covered her mouth. "That was—"

"Gunshots." Jordan released his hold on her. "Stay here."

To her horror, he sprinted across the grass, dodging between the raised grave markers. The wind shifted direction, blowing chilly rain against the side of the mausoleum. Within minutes, she was soaked. Her teeth chattered and shivers racked her body. As the time stretched out, her anxiety grew.

Making a decision, she set off after Jordan. Her heavy boots and the slick grass slowed her progress. The cemetery was enormous and hilly, and she had no way of knowing which direction he'd gone once she'd lost sight of him.

"Look for his footprints," she muttered to herself.

He was running and the ground was soft. She crisscrossed between the flattened markers until she discovered his deep depressions.

Rain pelted her back and drizzled down her neck. As she crested the hill, she slowed. The vantage point gave her a wide overview of the area, but there was no sign of Jordan, and the rain was filling in his footsteps.

A lone chapel was nestled at the bottom of the hill. The building appeared deserted, and as far as she knew, it hadn't been used in years.

Was he inside? Surely it was locked, but he had to be here someplace. The chapel was the logical choice.

Something white ricocheted off a cement bench to her left with a chink. The sound repeated itself. Soon more bits of white showered from the sky. Sleet.

With icy pellets stinging her skin, she dashed for the chapel. The sleet fell faster, bouncing off the grass and sounding against the grave markers. While her coat protected her arms, the tiny projectiles pummeled her face.

She doubted the chapel was open, but at least the covered porch might offer some protection.

Taking the stairs two at a time, she skidded to a halt before the ornate double doors, then took a moment to catch her breath. One of the doors was ajar.

Slowly edging it wider, she peered cautiously inside. The stale scent of dust and disuse assailed her. She pressed the door wider and hit something solid.

"Jordan?"

Her stomach lurched.

His eyes staring sightlessly at the ceiling, a man lay sprawled on the white marble in a growing pool of red.

His clothing indicated he was one of the men from the van.

NINE

Jordan eased Lucy away. "Don't look."

He'd meant to secure the door and save her from the grisly sight. He hadn't expected the weather to take such a nasty turn.

She wrapped her arms around him and buried her face against his shoulder. "Is the other one…?"

"I don't know." Jordan rested his cheek on the top of her head. "I didn't see anyone else. I don't know if the second man got away or if he's the shooter. The dead man doesn't have any identification."

He was babbling and he didn't normally babble. Her coat was soaked, and she trembled against him. Sleet bounced against the stained glass windows.

Everything in the chapel was covered with a fine layer of dust, and the air was musty and uncirculated. The place had the appearance of being frozen in time. There was an open book on the lectern and the charred stump of a candle on the altar. The walls were tiled in ornate pictures of angels, and the words *Until the day break and shadows flee away* circled the room's soffits in gold-painted relief.

"This isn't the man I saw when his mask came loose," she said. "He doesn't have a tattoo."

"We don't have to think about that now." Jordan guided her to a pew as far away from the body as the tiny chapel allowed. "Because this has changed from a kidnapping to a murder, I've called the police. They should be here soon."

She sat beside him and stared sightlessly at the altar, her hands tucked in her lap. He reached for them and rubbed her chilled fingers.

"You're freezing," he said.

"I don't even feel it."

He released her hands and took off his coat, then draped the material around her shoulders, drawing the front closed. Lucy grasped the edges and pulled them together. Her skin was unnaturally pale, making the blue of her eyes appear even brighter with her unshed tears.

After a moment, she bowed her head. "I'm going to say a prayer for him."

Jordan stretched his arm across her shoulders. He didn't know what to say or how to comfort her, so he sat in silence.

No words came to him. His prayers had been

empty since the day of the bombing. He still had faith and still went through the motions, but something had been missing. He'd thought time might give him perspective, but months had passed, and the void had not been filled.

His physical wounds had healed. He'd gone through rehab for his body, but the damage to his soul had never fully closed. Though he'd tried, he'd never been able to wholly identify the source of his restlessness—to put his finger on what was missing. There was only a vague, underlying sense of unease.

The doctors had counseled him about survivor's guilt and encouraged him to talk to a professional, but he hadn't felt the need. Everyone had lost something that day. He'd survived when others had not, and nothing was going to change that. While he recognized his own guilt surrounding his inability to prevent the tragedy, he wasn't one to wallow in self-pity. Dwelling on his own suffering was a betrayal to those people who'd lost everything.

Agonizing over whether or not he might have done something different that day served no purpose. There was no going back and changing what had happened. There was no point in wondering if he might have stopped the bombing if he'd gotten there sooner. That kind of thinking was pointless and circular.

The questions that *did* haunt him weren't easily answered. How had the surveillance equipment they'd planted been discovered? Why hadn't the bomber waited for Jordan's return? Those concerns preoccupied him because the answers had consequences that reverberated throughout his fieldwork. If they'd made a mistake once, what was preventing that same mistake from happening again?

Sirens sounded in the distance, and Lucy raised her head. Her storm-colored eyes were puffy.

She clutched his hand. "What do you think happened here?"

"I don't know." Jordan shook his head. "I don't know."

Living under intense pressure, he'd trained himself to focus on the problem and not his feelings. In the field, everyone worked with single-minded attention to the mission. Since seeing Lucy in person that first day in the coffee shop, the emotions he'd learned to ignore refused to be silent.

She rubbed her eyes, and the sleeves of his coat slipped down. Dark bruises mottled the skin of her wrists where she'd been bound.

He traced a finger over the discolored skin. "Does it hurt?"

Shaking her head, she dropped her arms and

yanked the cuffs over the bruises. "No. It probably looks worse than it is."

The next instant, she bolted upright and swiveled toward him, then gently touched his stomach. "Your ribs. They kicked you. Are you all right?"

He placed his hand over hers. "Nothing broken, I think."

When she touched him, his thoughts scattered. Her hair fell like a curtain in front of her face, and he ached to brush the strands aside. He wanted to see the peekaboo highlights.

"Are you sure?" She lifted her face, and her lips trembled. "Does it hurt to breathe?"

Gently brushing her hand away, he shook his head. "It's all right."

His ribs ached and his head throbbed. He felt as though he'd spent the past hour in a rock tumbler. It wasn't nearly as bad as waking up in the hospital after the bombing, but he'd had better days, that was for sure.

Ignoring him, she slid her fingers through his hair, her gentle touch gliding over the painful lump on the back of his head. When he looked at those lips, all thoughts of his aches and pains fled.

She sucked in a breath and leaned forward. "You might have a concussion."

"Maybe. Probably not."

Scooting closer, she ran her fingers through his hair, parting the strands. He covered her hand, preventing her from seeing the scar.

"Let me," she said softly.

The captivating moment passed, and a sense of panic gripped him. He moved away.

"I don't need your pity, Lucy." He brushed his hair back into place. "Leave it."

"You don't understand."

He glanced away. "Can we talk about something else? Like the fact that there's a dead guy over there and the police are about thirty seconds away. I think that takes precedence over a lump on my head."

In his panic, he didn't care that he was being a jerk. He wanted to escape her scrutiny by any means necessary. He didn't want her to see him as weak.

Relentless, she moved closer to him as he backed away, forcing him against the far side of the pew.

"Why isn't it okay for me to feel compassion? Why can't I feel sorrow for what you've suffered?"

"You can feel whatever you want." He stood and retreated, needing to put some distance between them. His chest ached and he pressed his fist against his sternum. "But it's wasted. I don't want your sympathy. I'm fine."

"Why not? You didn't deserve what happened to you."

"Great." He shook his head. "Not you, too. This isn't about survivor's guilt. Everyone who's ever taken a psychology course in college wants to make an amateur diagnosis. Not everything is complicated. I got hurt. I healed. End of story. It's simple."

The sound of the sirens grew louder, and he focused on the stained glass window. There was no fresh air in the building, and the walls were closing in on him.

Lucy stood. "I'm not trying to diagnose you. I'm sorry for what happened, that's all. I'm sorry for what you had to go through."

She reached for him and he jerked away.

"The police are almost here," he said. "They'll want to secure the scene. Keep track of where you've walked and what you've touched. They need that information for the forensics team."

"Okay."

He made the mistake of looking at her, and the pain in her beautiful eyes kicked him straight in the gut.

"They're here now," he said. The sounds of car doors slamming indicated the arrival of the authorities. "I'll let them know what happened. It's going to be another long day."

She took off his coat and tossed it over the back of the pew. "I'm ready."

The gesture felt symbolic. He'd pushed her away, and she was proving she didn't need him. Maybe it was better this way. There was no time for an apology, which he didn't want to say even if they weren't about to be swarmed by law enforcement.

She smoothed her hair, and he caught sight of the bruising on her wrists once more.

His training deserted him. This case didn't have an easy solution, and he was scared. He'd already failed Brandt. If something happened to Lucy, he'd never forgive himself.

Who was he kidding?

He was more than scared—he was terrified.

Seated by herself, Lucy studiously avoided looking behind her. She felt as though she was in a scene from a movie. She was the figure who remained stationary while everyone hurried around her.

The police had asked her several questions before largely ignoring her. The shattered screen had rendered her phone worthless, and she was forced to sit in silence while everyone worked.

Without a distraction, she stewed in her own troubled thoughts. How long had it been since she'd faced boredom without a crutch? Even now, many of the people who crowded the scene were hunched over their phones. Such an incongruous sight. There was a dead man not fifteen feet away, and one of the uniformed officers was texting. Life went on.

The conversation with Jordan played like a loop in her head. The more she thought about his accusations, the more confused she became. She hadn't been trying to diagnose him. When they'd talked in the van, he'd been open and honest about his injuries. In the chapel, he'd become defensive.

She'd done nothing wrong, and his reaction hurt her. As the emotion blossomed through her chest, her lips parted, and she dragged in a ragged breath.

Something broke loose inside her. For the past year, she'd been numb. She'd pushed all of her feelings aside and concentrated on the day-to-day. While she hadn't felt the pain, she hadn't felt the joy, either.

She'd thought the suffering was hers and hers alone. Now she wasn't as certain. Maybe if she hadn't been so distracted for the past year, she wouldn't have made such an easy target.

Someone had done this to her on purpose. Someone she worked with day in and day out had put her life in danger. The realization was sobering. She'd considered each of her coworkers in turn and had failed to settle on a single person she thought capable of something like this.

As she mentally walked through the list once more, she couldn't shake the feeling that she'd missed something important.

TEN

For the second time in the past three days, Jordan found himself surrounded by lights and sirens and police.

The man's body had been cordoned off behind screens while evidence was collected. The scene playing out was eerily similar to the events at the coffee shop only days before. Like actors in a play that ran night after night, they were all going through their same lines and hitting their same marks.

Westover, Karp and the two additional team members had taken seats in the front two pews. Lucy sat behind them, a silver blanket wrapped around her shoulders.

She must be freezing. The temperature had dropped along with the sleet and rain, and she'd gotten soaked in the process. Not once had she complained. Not once had she shown any signs of impatience.

A detective Jordan recognized from the coffee shop shooting approached him. He was tall and lanky with two deep vertical creases in his forehead that pulled his eyebrows together, giving him a perpetually cranky appearance. From what Jordan had seen, the detective knew his job. He'd kept the scene organized and professional.

"I'm Detective Ryan." The man stuck out his hand. "We met before."

Jordan accepted the proffered handshake. "Yeah. I remember."

"They found the van a few miles away from here," the detective said. "It was reported stolen a week ago. I'll have Forensics sweep the interior. Looks like there was blood on the driver's seat. Your second guy was injured. Might be a bullet wound. We'll know if he shows up at any of the local hospitals."

"You think they turned on each other and only one of them survived?"

"Maybe. There was mud in the parking lot, and we managed to save two sets of tire tracks. Can't really tell when the second set was left because of the sleet. If it's from a second car, we could be looking at an ambush. I'm pulling all the recordings from the entrance cameras in the cemetery just in case. But don't get your hopes up. Looks like at least one of the security cameras was vandalized recently. Doesn't take much to connect the dots."

Jordan considered the possibilities. Maybe the cemetery was the destination all along. The men were supposed to deliver Lucy to the chapel, but they messed up when they snatched Jordan, as well. If that was the case, there was a chance the buyer had shown his displeasure with a bullet.

"Then you haven't ruled out the possibility of a third party?" Jordan asked.

"Until we find the suspect with the tattoo, we won't know for sure what happened here." The detective gestured. "Thank you for securing the scene. Much appreciated."

"No problem."

The detective retrieved a business card from his breast pocket. "If you need any help, I can be ready on a moment's notice. If what you suspect is true, we've got a dead man walking out there. The sooner we find him, the better."

"I appreciate that."

Having already given his statement, Jordan made his way down the aisle and took the seat next to Lucy.

Westover said something that made her smile. She turned, and he knew the instant she saw him. Her smile faded and the sparkle in her eyes was replaced by a shuttered expression.

His gut clenched. He knew better than to get

defensive, but he'd gone and done it anyway. He'd apologize later, when they didn't have an audience.

He hesitated only a moment before slipping onto the pew beside her.

"How are you holding up?" he asked.

She tucked a strand of platinum hair behind one ear, her expression wary. "I've been better. Have you discovered anything new?"

He sincerely hoped he hadn't botched things between them for good. It wasn't Lucy's fault he'd let his temper get the better of him.

With the rest of the team staring at him expectantly, Jordan filled them in on everything he'd learned. When he finished, Karp retrieved a handkerchief from his pocket and removed his glasses.

"What about you guys?" Jordan asked. "What happened?"

As he absently polished the lenses, Karp said, "We got the video and audio of the kidnapping and set up a perimeter. Didn't take too long to figure out they'd slipped the net."

Westover planted his elbows on his knees and clasped his hands before him. "We found the sunglasses and your gun. We followed the tire tracks out of the park, but we lost them when they got to the road. What happened before that?"

"It was me," Jordan said. "They didn't count on someone interrupting them. Lucy had the foresight to say I was a friend she'd brought along for protection."

"Good thinking." Karp jabbed his thumb over his shoulder. "Or you'd be lying alongside that guy."

Her face pale, Lucy cast a surreptitious glance at the cordoned-off area. "I don't get it. Why kill him?"

"I don't know." Jordan stared at the portrait of an elaborate angel created from tiny square tiles on the chapel wall. "We have to consider two possibilities. Either these guys turned on each other, or whoever hired them wanted to clean up a few loose ends. Either way, at least one of the witnesses escaped. They found blood in the van."

"The buyer may want us to believe they turned on each other," Karp said. "There's a possibility he wanted to stage it that way, but one of them got away. Let's hope we can find him alive—otherwise, this is all empty conjecture."

"What do we do now?" Lucy asked.

"Let's get you out of here," Jordan said with a weary sigh. "Then we tell the buyer you're not interested in making any deals after today. End of story."

She tilted her head. "But doesn't that defeat the purpose of everything we've done?"

Karp replaced his glasses. The sparkling lenses reflected the harsh floodlights the police had set up to illuminate the scene.

"This has escalated," Karp said. "Ms. Sutton is in danger no matter what we do from this point out. I've been tracking the buyer for two years. He's never killed before. Something is different, and I don't like when people go off script. Makes me nervous. Something has him desperate, and that's not good for any of us. He's not going to stop until he gets what he wants."

"It's too risky for a civilian," Jordan said.

He hadn't been able to shake the image of the man grabbing Lucy by the hood of her coat and dragging her backward. They'd both gotten out alive—this time. They might not be as fortunate the next time around.

"This *is* dangerous," Lucy said. "I get it. I'm not stupid. But the buyer doesn't want me dead. He's had plenty of chances to kill me and he hasn't. That defeats his purpose."

"Look at that guy." Jordan jerked his chin toward the front of the chapel. "You don't have to look far to see what happens when someone doesn't suit his needs anymore."

Lucy scooted forward. "But we're not there yet. I'm still valuable. Plus, he thinks I have an overprotective boyfriend. Which means Jordan can be seen with me. This guy has heard us together in the house. He took a picture of us. He'll expect me to be with Jordan. It's the perfect cover for a bodyguard. After today, we can refuse to meet in person again. He can't fault us for that. That gives us leverage."

"She's right," Karp said. "But for now, we wait. He's got the flash drive. We see where that gets him."

"We also have his connection to Consolidated Unlimited," Westover added. "Jordan is cleared for employment. Someone tried to sell classified information, and they nearly succeeded. We find them, and we have another path to the buyer."

Lucy nodded. "Jordan and I can go to work like normal on Monday."

None of this struck Jordan as a good idea, and their current track record was abysmal. They'd put Lucy in danger, and they were no closer to discovering the identity of the buyer than they had been three days ago. One of the abductors was dead, and the other one had gone underground.

Karp glanced around. "Looks like they're wrapping up here. Westover and I will coordinate with the detective in charge and bring the car around. Jordan, why don't you stay with Ms. Sutton?"

Karp stood without waiting for an answer, leaving Jordan in the awkward position of being alone with Lucy once more.

Clearing his throat, he stared at his clasped hands. "I'm sorry. About before. I don't know what came over me."

"It's all right. It's been a long day. I think we're both entitled to be a little cranky."

Her hair was damp, dragging the waves almost straight, and the cut on her cheek stood out in harsh relief to her pale skin.

"I shouldn't have taken it out on you," he said. "I'm sorry for that."

"Apology accepted."

"Just like that?"

"Yes." A smile danced around the corners of her mouth. "Just like that. Forgiveness is much easier than carrying a grudge, and I've always been lazy."

"I highly doubt that." Despite the events of the day, he felt as though a weight had been lifted off his chest. "We'll figure out what happened here. I promise you that."

He'd put her life in danger, and she deserved to know the risk wasn't in vain.

Detective Ryan lumbered down the aisle and

paused beside Jordan. "You guys know anything about this?"

He held up an evidence bag with a smashed flash drive, and Jordan's heart sank.

Despite everything they'd done, they were back to square one.

Lucy checked her reflection in the mirror and considered changing her dress, then stopped herself. This was ridiculous. She wasn't going on a first date; she was going to her job. There was no reason to be this worked up and excited. She was being ridiculous.

Even with all her self-talk, her heart beat a rat-a-tat-tat in her chest.

True to his word, Jordan's team had rented the house next door, and Jordan was living there full-time. Over the weekend, they'd set up both video and audio surveillance equipment. They'd swept her house and discovered only listening devices, which they'd identified for Lucy. There were two on the first level and one in her office.

Knowing the devices were there had annoyed her the first day, but she'd grown accustomed to them in a remarkably short amount of time. When she was alone, they rarely bothered her. She hadn't even curtailed her off-key singing, and she hoped her unwelcome listeners were heartily annoyed. She'd even added "Don't Rain on My Parade" to the rotation, and she couldn't hit any of the notes in that song.

To maintain their cover, Jordan had come over two nights in a row. On Saturday she'd made dinner, and on Sunday he'd brought take-out. While they studiously shunned personal details in deference to their remote audience, they'd gotten to know each other's favorite books and movies. Following the incident in the chapel, she'd been careful to avoid any mention of his injuries.

Of all the inconveniences she'd suffered over the past week, having a fake boyfriend wasn't the worst thing that had happened.

Fifteen minutes later, she opened the door for Jordan.

She'd changed her dress. Not out of vanity, of course. Only because it was supposed to be warmer today than the day before. If she thought the style was better suited to her figure, that was merely a coincidence.

Jordan clapped his hands. "Ready to face corporate America?"

For the first day on the job, he'd dressed in business casual with navy trousers and a fitted blue button-up shirt. The slight hint of cologne drifting through the open door sent her heartbeat into overdrive.

"Ready," she replied, only slightly breathless.

As far as anyone from Consolidated Unlimited was concerned, Lucy had recommended her friend and neighbor for a job in the department. The ruse allowed her and Jordan to carpool without anybody questioning their prior relationship.

Jordan offered to drive, and she gladly accepted.

When they turned onto the main road, she smoothed the material of her dress over her knees. "Maybe I should change my hair color."

Her cheeks flamed. *Great.* She hadn't meant to blurt that out quite so abruptly. They'd gotten to know each other over the past few days, and she sensed he'd give her an honest opinion.

Jordan glanced at her from the corner of his eye. "Why would you do that?"

"Someone obviously thought it was easy to impersonate me because of my hair." She'd been thinking about her mom's advice all week. Maybe it was time to listen. "And the way I dress. What if I was—I don't know—more normal? Would it be more difficult to impersonate me?"

"You don't have to change anything. Not unless you want to. Do you want to?"

"I don't know. Would it be better if I looked more mainstream?"

"You look normal to me already."

"But I have blue highlights. And it's not just about someone impersonating me. Consolidated Unlimited is a conservative company. It's not a cutting-edge tech start-up in San Francisco. What if I get passed over for a promotion because of my hair?" Her mom had harped on the possibility often enough. "I want to be taken seriously. I'd hate to think that how I dress is holding me back from job opportunities."

"Not according to your supervisor, it's not. He did nothing but sing your praises during my interview."

She blew out a breath. "That's good to hear."

"Times are different these days. Part of my job involves the ability to blend into a crowd. To go unnoticed. Being invisible is good for what I do, but it's not necessarily an asset in the corporate world. Besides, you're pretty tame compared to what I see other people wearing. You don't even have tattoos or piercings. And I like your hair."

Her stomach flipped. "You do?"

She hadn't been fishing for a compliment, but she didn't mind getting one.

"Your hair is cool. And I'm not just saying that. I like that you take risks. I like every— I like that you take risks. As long as you do good work and take your job seriously, other people will, too."

She couldn't quite tell, but she thought maybe he'd blushed a little. Maybe she'd make a few small changes and meet her mom's advice in the middle. She'd still be Lucy, just a polished version.

Sensing she was making him uncomfortable, she changed the subject. "Is it weird? Working in an office like a regular joe?"

"Hate to break it to you, but I *am* a regular joe. When I'm not in the field, I'm sitting in a cubicle in Maryland. It's not that different."

He turned into the parking lot and flashed his credentials to the security guard in the booth.

Frank leaned out of the sliding glass window. "Hey, Lucy. Haven't seen you in a couple of days. Hope you're feeling better."

"Much better," she said, stretching over Jordan to wave at the friendly security guard. "Thank you."

Given the awkward angle, she had to press her hand against Jordan's thigh to resume her seat. She quickly retracted her arm, though she couldn't help noticing his well-developed muscles. Clearly he was a runner. Probably he had to stay in shape given his job. Maybe he'd be interested in doing a little biking this week. Just to maintain their cover, of course.

"This must be the new guy," Frank said, waving them through. "Pleasure to meet you, sir."

"You, too."

"Don't forget your credentials," Frank called after them. "Or I can't let you in. No exceptions. I always remind the new guys."

Jordan sketched a wave. "Got it."

Lucy hadn't thought she'd be nervous about returning to work, but now that she was here, her hands were clammy and the muscles along her shoulders ached. Someone inside that building had nearly gotten her killed. Did they understand the havoc they'd wreaked on her life? Did they care?

Jordan pulled into a parking space and killed the engine. "Remember, pay close attention to everything that happens in there. Anything that's out of the ordinary. Anyone who's acting strangely. Even someone who's being overly friendly. Even if somebody is avoiding you. Both things could be signs of guilt."

Lucy waved her hand between them. "What about us?"

The phrase was much more suggestive than she'd intended, and she ducked her head, letting her hair fall like a curtain over her face.

"We're friends. You don't have to treat me any differently than you normally would. Just don't mention my connection to Brandt."

The reference to Brandt sobered her. Lately she'd gone for longer and longer stretches of time without thinking about him. He was always there, in the back of her mind, but other thoughts had taken precedence.

"Okay," she replied. "We're neighbors. We're friends. Got it."

Jordan was remarkably relaxed. From what little she'd learned about his job while she was with Brandt, they monitored communications from hostile foreign governments and extremist groups. Brandt had always downplayed the danger. He'd once told her a story about tracking the vibrations in a house for weeks on end. When he said his job was boring, she'd believed him.

Then she'd read an article about how the National Security Agency had captured a terrorist. They'd monitored the compound for weeks, tracking the vibrations, until they'd discovered one of the occupants never left the compound. His boring job hadn't seemed quite so boring after that. She should have realized that his work was more dangerous than he let on.

"You look terrified." Jordan reached into the back seat for her lunch box. "You're supposed to be relaxed. As though everything is normal. Just be yourself. I'll be right there with you. I won't let anything happen."

"I know you won't let anything happen to me." How did she explain that her expression had nothing to do with terror and everything to do with their relationship? Despite all that had happened, the weekend had been remarkably uneventful. Spending time with Jordan was a pleasure, and she didn't know whether to feel guilty or exhilarated or both. "Should we have lunch together? It's your first day. I'd probably have lunch with a friend on their first day."

"Perfect. I'll meet you in the break room at noon. I won't see much of you this morning. I have to attend orientation like any other employee. Otherwise, it will look suspicious."

"I hope you like coffee." She chuckled. "Orientation is torturously boring."

"Not gonna lie. I'm not looking forward to it."

Despite having a top secret security clearance and working for a government contractor, Lucy didn't know much about undercover work. She also didn't know what to make of what was happening between them. While she recognized that pieces of their relationship were exaggerated fiction, other parts of their time together felt remarkably authentic.

He reached for the door, and she grasped his forearm. "Is any of this real to you? Because… because I've enjoyed getting to know you. Are we friends?"

His expression sobered. Cupping the back of her head, he drew her closer, then planted a kiss on her forehead. At the gentle touch of his lips, the world slipped away for a moment.

"How can you doubt that?" he asked.

He pulled away and she leaned in. Her heart pounded with uncertainty. More than his words of reassurance, she wanted to kiss him. She needed to feel if what was happening between them was real or all part of a show.

His lips parted, whether in question or to stop her, she didn't know. Taking advantage of his brief hesitation, she pressed her mouth against his.

For a moment he didn't move. Then his hands lifted to her cheeks in a gentle caress. He murmured something unintelligible and deepened the kiss, his fingers sliding down her back. His touch ignited the tiny spark of hope that had been flickering inside her. She angled her head and he pulled her closer. As she drank in the feel of him, warmth curled inside her.

"We can't." He pulled away abruptly, putting some space between them though his arms were still wrapped around her. "This isn't right, Lucy."

Her chest rose and fell with her rapid breathing. If she pressed her hand against his heart, she was certain she'd discover it was beating as rapidly as hers.

"Jordan."

His hands dropped away and he turned from

her. "We better get going. Can't be late on my first day."

Suddenly bereft, she glanced around, grateful there was no one else in the parking lot. At least no one had seen them. She'd be mortified if word of them canoodling in the car wound up as watercooler fodder.

Clearly she was in over her head and in danger of drowning. She'd felt his response, yet he'd turned away. She was confused and didn't understand the rules of their relationship. Apparently, neither did Jordan. While that should have comforted her, his contradictory behavior left her isolated and alone.

Another car pulled into the lot, and she recognized one of her coworkers. It was time to resume the show.

"Lucy, relax," Jordan admonished gently.

"I am relaxed."

"It was just a kiss."

She turned away before her expression revealed her thoughts. No. He hadn't felt the same thing at all. For him, *it was just a kiss*.

They'd been together too much this past week, that was all. She needed some space. Maybe once she got back to work and returned to her normal routine, the feelings would fade.

Jordan stepped out of the car, and together they strolled into the building as though nothing had happened. Once inside, she gave him directions to Human Resources for his intake.

As she stared at his retreating back, he turned. When his eyes met hers, Lucy's heart skipped a beat, and everything seemed to be in slow motion. She'd wanted to know if what was happening between them was real, and now she had her answer.

He wasn't indifferent to her, no matter how much he tried to pretend otherwise.

The question remained. What was she going to do about it?

ELEVEN

Two weeks after starting his undercover job with Lucy, Jordan found himself outside the base chapel on a Saturday afternoon. Lucy was with the police going through yet another set of mug shots while Jordan had returned to finish up some loose ends on the project that had brought him to Omaha in the first place.

His team had completed the tasks in record time, and he'd gone for a run. For reasons he couldn't explain, his path had led him to the chapel. He glanced down and caught sight of his running shoes. Even if he had an explanation for how he'd wound up here in the first place, he wasn't exactly dressed for church. As he turned away, someone opened the door.

Jordan tottered backward to avoid a collision and met the man's startled gaze.

"Sorry about that," the man apologized. "Didn't see you there." He held the door with one hand. "Going inside?"

"No, no." Jordan swiped at the perspiration on his forehead. "I was just out for a run. I'm not exactly dressed to go inside."

"I'm the chaplain, Pastor Byrne. Most folks just call me Chaplain." He stuck out his hand. "Pleasure to meet you."

Jordan shook the proffered hand and introduced himself.

Pastor Byrne was tall and tan with a large forehead and steel-gray hair that matched his eyes. His black suit and jacket hung loosely off his lanky frame, and his black leather shoes reflected the afternoon sunlight.

He rocked back on his heels. "If you have need of the chapel, I have it on good authority there's no dress code."

Shaking his head, Jordan said, "It's all right. I don't need anything."

"You've lost someone, haven't you?"

"Yes." The question caught him off guard, and Jordan's throat constricted. "How did you know?"

"You do this job long enough, you get an instinct about things." The chaplain clasped his hands behind his back. "I was going for a walk. Care to join me?"

"No. I can't. I should be getting back."

Despite his protests, Jordan hesitated. He felt as

though a great pressure was building inside him, and if he didn't talk to someone, he'd explode.

"Things happen in this world we don't always have the answers for." The chaplain spoke quietly. "I see a lot of grief in this job. A lot of loss. Senseless loss. We look to God in those times, and sometimes He answers by sending us the people we need to guide us."

Something had led Jordan here this morning. His meeting had wrapped up earlier than he'd expected. His run had taken him on a different route than normal. The chaplain had been leaving just when he got here. A half-dozen small steps had led him to this place.

Instead of fighting, he'd choose to see the wisdom in the chaplain's words.

He hesitated another moment, then said, "Sure. I have time for a walk." He checked his phone before stowing it in his pocket once more. No messages. "I'm not stationed here. I'm a contractor."

"I thought your hair was a little too long for regulation."

Jordan ran his fingers through the length. "Yeah. I'm due for a haircut."

"But not too short, I'm guessing. You don't want anyone to know the extent of your injuries, do you?"

Jordan stopped in his tracks.

The pastor halted a few paces ahead of him and held up his hand. "Like I said, you get an instinct for these things. This person you lost, was he killed in the same accident?"

"Yes," Jordan replied, his voice hoarse. "A buddy of mine. We worked together. In Pakistan. There was a bombing."

"I'm sorry for your loss."

"We got to be friends. It was about a year ago. Sometimes it feels like it was a million years ago, and sometimes it feels as though it was yesterday."

The pastor resumed walking. "Tell me about him."

At a momentary loss, Jordan considered his answer. No one had ever asked such a pointed question. People generally understood what to say when a family member died. When a friend died, the rules were different. The language wasn't as established. He felt as though he'd lost a brother, but he hadn't. Instead of trying to explain to people, he'd stayed silent.

The chaplain was patiently waiting for his answer, and Jordan said the first things that came to mind. "He was larger than life. Funny. Smart. A good friend. He had a beautiful fiancée. He had everything."

"I wish I'd met him."

"You'd have liked him. Everyone did." Jordan

cleared his throat. "He wasn't perfect, don't get me wrong. We both made plenty of mistakes. That's the thing. We were young and stupid together, and I wanted to see us when we were old and wise."

"Sounds like your friend had a blessed life ahead of him."

"He did." Jordan ached for the kind of love Brandt had found. What would it be like to have someone like Lucy love him unconditionally? To find a partner to spend the rest of his life with. He couldn't even imagine. "Brandt had found peace. I'd never seen him so happy. He'd have made a great husband. A great dad."

Jordan's attempts at speaking with his own dad about the loss were futile. His dad had been raised during a time when men didn't speak about their feelings, and he was uncomfortable with emotion—especially from his son. He wasn't an insensitive man—he simply didn't know how to speak about those kinds of things, so he remained silent. A trait Jordan had learned to utilize on occasion, as well.

"What about you?" the chaplain asked. "Do you see those things in your future? Marriage? Children?"

"I don't know anymore." Pressure built behind Jordan's eyes. "Since the bombing, everything feels temporary. I don't know how to explain it. Everything feels so close to the end. If your life can be taken from you in an instant, what's the point of planning for a future? I know it's not logical, but that's how it feels."

"When have feelings ever been logical?" The pastor stepped beneath the shade of a crabapple tree and leaned his shoulder against the trunk, then crossed his arms. "I'll bore you with the abbreviated version of the speech I give returning soldiers. It goes something like this. In the field, you're trained to control human instinct and emotion toward one goal—completion of the mission. The effects of living in that state while navigating a hostile environment are both biological and physiological. When someone dies in the field, that mission feels incomplete. The sense of unfinished business complicates the grieving process, even under the best of circumstances. And most deaths overseas are complicated."

"That's just it, though. I haven't earned this grief. I have no right to it." Jordan felt his chin wobble and hated the show of weakness. "I wasn't his brother. I was only his friend. I don't have a right to feel this way."

"You have every right." For the first time, a thread of steel ran through the chaplain's voice. "We have the family we are born with and the family we choose. Neither is more significant than the other."

Jordan studied the tops of his running shoes. "I suppose you're right. We were as close as family." Dappled sunlight filtering through the tree leaves created shimmering patterns on the grass. "I didn't realize how much I still miss him until recently."

Why were these feelings surfacing now? He'd grieved. His physical wounds had healed. Then he'd finally screwed up the courage to give Lucy the ring, and something had shifted inside him. He missed having someone he trusted when he was in the field.

Everyone assumed he had survivor's guilt, and while there was a thread of truth in that, the reality was far more complex. He wasn't a cliché. There was no point in wondering why he had survived and Brandt had not. Some questions didn't have answers. Why, then, had this void opened inside him?

"There are no rules to mourning." The chaplain spoke into the silence. "We'd all like to believe there are five clear stages, and once we've navigated them, the grieving is over. Loss isn't like that. There are no rules. We cycle in and out, and sometimes we even get snagged in one stage and can't break free. That's when we need help to get unstuck."

Jordan hadn't realized how much he'd kept bottled inside until now. The surgeon had urged him to talk to a professional because that was par for the course when an agent was injured in the field. He'd ignored the suggestion. Then Lucy kissed him, and his feelings had been churned up again. Everything was jumbled inside him: sorrow, loss, guilt and—somewhere in the mix—a desperate sense of longing.

"Is there something else?" The chaplain curled his thumb and forefinger against his lips. "I sense there's something troubling you beyond the loss of your friend. I can assure you, there's very little I haven't heard during my time in this job. I'm not here to judge."

Maybe it was because he was speaking to the chaplain that Jordan was compelled to confess what had been bothering him the most this past week.

He sucked in a breath and plunged ahead. "I've been spending time with Brandt's fiancée. Not romantically. It's, well, it's hard to explain. She's the only other person who understands what I'm feeling. But when I'm with her, I feel like I'm living another man's life."

"Are you in love with her?" At Jordan's shocked expression, the chaplain only smiled. "You made a point of saying that you weren't seeing her romantically. Makes me think you'd like to."

Jordan's chest ached because he wasn't ready to admit he had those kinds of thoughts about her. Not out loud. Not to another person. He didn't even want to admit those feelings to himself. She wasn't his, and she never had been.

Not wanting to lie, he said, "I think I could."

He'd been well on his way to falling in love with her for some time. When Brandt was alive, his feelings had been harmless. She was funny, bright and pretty. What guy wouldn't like someone like that? Because of his friendship with Brandt, his affection for Lucy had been safe and contained. A bit of harmless fun. Those same feelings didn't seem harmless now.

The chaplain plucked a dangling leaf from the branch above him. "Would that be so bad? Falling in love?"

The blood rushed in Jordan's ears. "Yes. No. Maybe."

Acting on his feelings was a betrayal of everything he stood for. He prided himself on his loyalty, and that hadn't changed with Brandt's death.

"Your friend—"

"Brandt," Jordan supplied.

The chaplain resumed walking, his attention focused straight ahead. "You grieve Brandt because he was an important part of your life. You miss him deeply because he was woven into the fabric of who you are, and now the pattern has changed. When people mean that much to us, we can't help feeling profound pain. Perhaps the best thing we can do is dedicate ourselves to being a meaningful part of someone else's life. To pass along that gift. Because that's the beauty of joy, isn't it? It's best when it's shared."

They'd reached the end of the path, and Jordan glanced at his fitness watch. He'd promised Lucy he'd be home when she returned.

Just the thought of seeing her gave him butterflies. Actual butterflies like they talked about in books and movies. But if he gave in to his own feelings, he'd be placing Lucy in an impossible situation. He wasn't going to risk their friendship.

The chaplain turned in the direction of the chapel once more. "How long are you assigned at the base?"

"I don't know," Jordan replied, grateful for the change of subject. "Things are up in the air now. Maybe a couple more months. Then it's back to Maryland."

"Ah." The chaplain nodded. "You're with the National Security Agency. I should have guessed. Don't worry. Anything you say to me stays within the sanctity of the church."

Jordan recalled the ring wrapped in blue silk, and his thoughts grew troubled. He'd made a few discreet inquiries about the woman Brandt had been speaking with in the hotel lobby in Pakistan. Nothing had panned out. All of his leads had turned out to be dead ends.

"I have a question," Jordan began, unsure how to even phrase his concerns.

"Let's see if I have an answer."

There was nothing classified about the information, which meant there was no harm in asking for a little advice. "Brandt had a ring made in Islamabad while we were there. It was an exact replica of the one his fiancée is wearing. He'd said he was going to propose to her properly, but he'd already given her an identical ring. Why do you suppose he had a second ring made? Why did he lie about proposing to her properly if he already had?"

"Did you ask his fiancée about it?"

"No. I, uh, I haven't."

Jordan didn't want to voice his fears out loud. He'd known Brandt as well as anyone. He trusted him. Until he knew differently, there was no point in risking ugly rumors.

The chaplain knit his fingers together and pressed his knuckles against his chin. "I can see your dilemma. While there may be a perfectly innocent explanation, there also may not."

He lowered his arms and slipped his hands into his pockets. "I'd ask the jeweler. If your friend wanted a replica, he provided a copy of the original. And, I assume, some sort of explanation. I'd imagine a duplicate is a memorable request. Even if the explanation your friend gave was a lie, it should give you a clue."

Unable to contain his burgeoning excitement, Jordan clutched the chaplain's shoulders. "You're a genius. An absolute genius."

Why hadn't he thought of that before now? Probably because the day he discovered the ring was a duplicate was the same day of the coffee shop attack. He'd been going nonstop since then, and such a simple solution had never occurred to him.

"I've been called many things," the chaplain said with a smile. "I can't say that I've been called a genius. I could get used to that."

Jordan dropped his arms and jogged a few paces away before turning and running backward. "Thanks for the talk. And the advice."

He pivoted and made his way toward his car.

Hope stirred in his chest. After all this time, he finally had a decent lead.

TWELVE

As the time neared noon, Lucy tapped her foot impatiently. She and Jordan generally ate lunch together, except his fake job had gotten a little too real lately. He'd been consulting on an assignment on the other side of the building for nearly a week.

She hadn't spent any time alone with Jordan for days. In the evenings, to avoid the listening devices, she'd gone to the house next door. Together with at least one other person, they'd pored over the Facebook pages and photos of fellow employees, searching for anyone of Lucy's height and build who might be connected to someone in the building.

Since the kiss, Jordan had become polite but distant.

She straightened the papers on her desk, revealing a photo of Brandt.

There was sadness in seeing him, but other emotions were surfacing, as well. When he'd said he was going to be stationed overseas for an extended period of time, she'd felt something akin to desperation. She'd felt as though she was being abandoned. His proposal had been impulsive, and she'd shocked herself by saying yes. Making the decision had been both risky and exciting. She'd known the relationship was too new for such a momentous decision, but she'd been head over heels, and the risk had felt worth taking.

She didn't regret her decision. Their time together had been wonderful and transformative. She wasn't the same person she'd been when she met Brandt. She was better. Even though losing him had hurt more than she ever could have imagined, she had no regrets. As time passed, she'd been able to see the happiness as well as the pain. She'd come to accept that grief and joy often coexisted. She'd accepted that part of what she grieved was the future she'd planned on building with him.

Voices sounded and she straightened, planting her hands on her keyboard.

Her supervisor, Alan, appeared with Jordan in tow. "Lucy, I can't thank you enough for bringing this guy to our attention. He's already been an invaluable resource for the Greenspace project." Alan indicated the empty cubicle next to hers. "Since he's ready to tackle the next level, he'll be sitting next to you. Why don't you show him the ropes since he hasn't worked with your department yet?"

"I'll do that."

She caught Jordan looking at her before his gaze skittered away, and her heart sank. He'd been this way since she'd kissed him. The act had been spontaneous and, looking back, stupid. He'd responded and she was certain he'd felt something, too. Then he'd spent the past two weeks treating her as though they were strangers. He was polite and nice when they were forced to interact, but she feared she'd damaged their friendship beyond repair.

Alan dropped a stack of papers on the empty desk. "I'm going to introduce him to the rest of the Greenspace team in your department. When we get back, why don't you take him out to lunch?"

"Will do."

After they'd rounded the corner, Sue McGuiness peeked over the partition. "Now, there's a tall drink of water."

Sue was in her late forties with shoulder-length brown hair, a slightly plump figure and an open personality. She also had a husband and two teenage boys.

Lucy rolled her eyes. "You're married."

Sue scooted around the partition. "My body

may be on a diet, but my eyes are free to roam the buffet. And you're *not* married, so you can look all you want. It's time you got back out there."

Lucy nibbled on a thumbnail and glanced at Brandt's picture. "I don't know. It doesn't seem right."

Instantly contrite, Sue took the seat Alan had assigned to Jordan. "I didn't mean to rush you." She patted Lucy's hand. "Don't listen to me. Do whatever feels right."

"That's just it. I don't know how I feel." Jordan had put a lot of emphasis on the word *friend* after the kiss. He was clearly setting boundaries. Did he think her interest in him was a betrayal of Brandt? Was it? "Doesn't that make me shallow? To have two relationships a year apart?"

She'd had boyfriends before Brandt, but never anything serious. No one who had ever made her toes curl just thinking about him. Why, after all this time, had lightning chosen to strike twice this close together?

"You don't get an award for how long you mourn someone." Sue leaned forward. "It's not like you get one chance at happiness and that's it. We don't get to pick the timing. You're allowed to be *happy*." She glanced over Lucy's head. "Whoops. The boss is coming back. Wait a second—is this guy even single?"

"Yes. But he's my neighbor. We only know each other in passing. I don't want to make things awkward."

"Then get to know him better." Sue stood and leaned against the cubicle partition. "Borrow a cup of sugar. Borrow two. Borrow enough that he finally gets the message, then see what happens."

"I don't know. He doesn't think of me that way."

"Doesn't he?" Sue winked. "I'll keep an eye on him. By tomorrow, I'll know if he thinks of you *that way*. I can always tell."

"No," Lucy whispered. "You don't have to do that."

"My pleasure."

Before Lucy could protest further, Jordan appeared. "I've met the team. I guess this is where I'm sitting."

He held himself stiffly, and she stood, smoothing her skirt. "Be careful of the chair. We've ordered a new one."

"Sure thing."

An instant message from Sue appeared on her screen: He's totally hot for you.

Lucy quickly collapsed the box with Sue's message. "Do you like Chinese food? There's a great restaurant down the street. The service is fast, and we go there all the time."

"That sounds good."

Lucy peered over the partition. "Would you like to go with us, Sue?"

"Nope. Can't. Working through lunch today."

"Are you sure?"

"Positive."

Lucy reached for her purse, and her phone buzzed. A text from Sue appeared: I don't want to be a third wheel.

Lucy chose an emoji with the tongue sticking out and hit Send.

She reached for her purse and caught sight of her engagement ring. Casting a furtive glance over her shoulder, she slid it off and placed it in her wallet. Maybe he was confused because she'd been sending mixed messages.

Jordan played music in the car on the way to the restaurant, preventing any meaningful conversation. She sensed the last place he wanted to be was alone with her at lunch. To make matters worse, the waiter seated them in a cozy booth at the back of the restaurant before handing them two plastic-covered menus. Oriental fans and paper globes dangled from the ceiling, and the walls featured black-lacquered panels.

She hadn't meant for things to be awkward between them. She didn't doubt his feelings were as complicated as hers. She only wanted to know if there could be anything between them.

Lucy tucked a lock of hair behind one ear and pretended to study the menu while she gathered her courage.

As she formed the question in her mind, her stomach churned. "Jordan, about—"

"What do you recommend? The kung pao chicken looks good."

He was deflecting the topic once again. This had to stop. "If I promise not to kiss you again, will you at least look me in the eye?"

Lifting the menu, he blocked her view of his face. "Why don't we just pretend it never happened?"

A part of her wanted to agree. How much easier to simply go back to the way things were before? Except that would be a lie. Something had sparked between them, and there was no point in ignoring it.

She hooked her finger on the top of the menu and pulled it down. "You have never struck me as a coward."

He lowered his hands with a sigh. "I, uh, I shouldn't have kissed you back. I'm sorry. That's my fault."

My fault. As though there was someone to blame. Her palms grew damp and a thread of panic wound through her. She'd really gone and done it now. She'd read the signs totally wrong, and she'd made a colossal mess of everything. He didn't feel the same about her at all.

She was worse than a teenager with her first crush—thinking that if her feelings were this strong, his must be, too. But the signs had been there. He'd been trying to tell her he didn't feel the same way. What an idiot she was.

The waiter came and took their orders, and her thoughts raced. How was she going to extricate herself from this mess? She was hurt, but more than that, she was afraid. She valued his friendship, and now she'd gone and mucked it up.

When they were alone once more, she sucked in a sharp breath. "You know what? You're right. With everything that's going on, I got carried away. It was a mistake, like you said. We can pretend it never happened."

The stubborn part of her didn't want to give up. The practical part of her didn't want to become like one of those crazy stalkers in a Lifetime Movie. Sure, she'd always wonder if the spark between them was worth fanning into a flame, but the risk wasn't worth losing him forever. Besides, he'd taken the choice away from her.

He met her gaze and his eyes were filled with an emotion she couldn't fathom. "I'll be your friend. Always. But there can't be anything more between us."

His obvious relief sent her heart plunging.

"Okay," she offered brightly. "See how easy that was? It's water under the bridge. No big deal. We can go back to the way things were. Easy breezy."

He straightened his silverware. "Did you discover anything new while I was getting up to speed on the Greenspace project?"

The change of subject was abrupt and final. There'd be nothing more said on the matter. Easy breezy.

"Nothing. And I don't know where to look next. I even pored over pictures from the office Christmas party." She shivered. "It's weird, working with people, wondering who is involved."

"Westover says they found some footage of the car they think might belong to the buyer. One of the homes near the back entrance of the cemetery had a doorbell camera. The image isn't that great, but it may help us corroborate his involvement later."

"Have they found the second man yet? The man with the tattoo."

"No. Nothing yet."

Her eyes burned. She wanted to ask him why he couldn't love her. Instead, she kept her disappointment to herself. His reluctance might be because of Brandt. Then again, maybe she just wasn't his type. Either way, she'd rather have him as a friend than never see him again, and friendship was all he was offering.

Straightening her silverware, she avoided looking directly at Jordan. "I'm sure something will turn up soon."

She'd already lost one person she loved; she couldn't bear losing another.

As they exited the restaurant, Jordan scanned the parking lot, searching for anything out of place. It appeared as though everyone in the city was outside and enjoying the temperate spring weather.

Lucy walked briskly, weaving her way through the parked cars. She'd driven because she knew where the restaurant was located. He couldn't read her mood, but her body language suggested tension.

He'd thought the conversation in the restaurant had gone well, all things considered, but now he wasn't as certain. She paused at the side of her car and looked down. As she turned toward him, a truck pulled out, blocking his view. He waited impatiently for the truck to pass and jogged the distance to the car.

Lucy slid into the driver's seat. The light reflecting off the windows prevented him from seeing her clearly. He couldn't put his finger on the source of his unease, but he sensed something was wrong.

He opened the passenger door and froze.

There was a man sitting in the back seat, his gun trained on Lucy.

THIRTEEN

Jordan tightened his hold on the handle of the door.

"Get in," the man ordered.

His skin was blotched red and his dirty blond hair was matted. His black T-shirt was wrinkled and there were dark patches that might be blood on his worn jeans. He'd wound a length of red cloth around his thigh. This must be the man who'd escaped the shooting at the cemetery. Why was he here?

A dozen different options rocketed through Jordan's head, and he slid into the passenger seat.

Jordan kept his hands outstretched and visible and his expression neutral. "Why don't we all stay calm?"

"I am calm," the man declared, the barrel of his gun wavering. "Drive."

Lucy was pale, and her hands trembled on the steering wheel.

Jordan touched her arm. "It's all right."

She glanced at him, her eyes wide and frightened. "Where? Where do I drive?"

The man in the back seat bounced his knee. "Back to the cemetery. Drive back to the cemetery. You know where."

He turned and Jordan recognized the distinctive tattoo on his neck. It appeared as though the bullet had caught him in the thigh, and he hadn't been able to seek medical attention. There was no telling how much blood he'd lost.

The man was terrified, weak and unpredictable.

"What's this all about?" Jordan asked. The situation required a delicate hand. "Do you want money? We can get you money."

Cash was always a good place to start.

"Money wouldn't hurt." The man swiped at his nose with the back of his hand. "Who wants me dead, lady?"

Lucy cast a sharp glance over her shoulder. "I don't know what you're talking about. You kidnapped me. I should be asking you that question."

"You're telling me you don't know why someone wanted to hire me?"

"Hold it." Jordan raised his hands higher. "Hold it. Let's start at the beginning. Someone hired you. Who?"

"I don't know. That's just it. This was Jimmy's deal." Perspiration beaded the man's brow, and his hands trembled. "We were supposed to put pressure on this lady. That's all I know."

"What kind of pressure?" Jordan asked.

He focused his attention on Lucy, willing her to stay calm. The guy didn't want to kill them, and as long as they stayed in relative control of the situation, they had every chance of escaping this unharmed.

The man lifted the edge of his T-shirt and scrubbed at the sweat on his forehead. "She wasn't answering her texts. I was supposed to get her attention. Then she met with you." He waved his gun toward Jordan. "I thought maybe you was an undercover cop or something. You look like it, except for the hair. The hair is too long. I fired a few shots into the coffee shop. I figured if the Boy Scout here was working undercover, he'd have backup. Except only the regular guys showed up."

"Then you weren't aiming to kill?" Jordan asked, though he already knew the answer. He wanted to keep the guy talking—and distracted.

"Nah. We was just trying to scare her. Maybe see if she'd gone to the cops already. But she hadn't."

Lucy slowed the car for a red light. "Then you don't know who hired you?"

"That's what I said, lady. Ain't you listening? I don't know who hired me."

"Okay, okay." Jordan's thoughts raced. "Take it easy."

"You take it easy. You ain't the one with a price on your head."

The guy was pointing a gun at them, which put them in a dangerous situation. "Jimmy was obviously meeting someone at the chapel. What did you see that day?"

Jordan reached into his pocket and pulled out his phone. Keeping his attention on the guy in the back seat, he unlocked the screen.

"I didn't see anything. Jimmy wasn't supposed to bring anyone with him, so I was lying low in the van. Waiting. I heard the gunshots, and I panicked. Jimmy didn't have a gun, so I knew he wasn't the one doing the shooting."

Lucy caught sight of Jordan's phone on the seat and blanched.

She adjusted her sun visor, drawing the man's attention to her. "Then you didn't see anybody?"

Jordan used the distraction to hit Mute and dial Karp.

The man shook his head. "All I saw was that place getting smaller in my rearview mirror. I didn't stick around to ask questions."

Karp must have picked up the call, because

the screen changed to show the seconds ticking by.

Tenting his hand over the phone, Jordan swiveled in his seat. "We're taking you back to the cemetery, back to where Jimmy was shot. I heard you two arguing that day while we were in the back of the van. What was that all about?"

"We weren't supposed to bring you, but Jimmy didn't know what else to do. Killing you would draw too much attention. If we left you, and you called the cops before we ditched the van, we risked getting caught. So we threw you in the back. The guy who hired Jimmy didn't like the change in plans. Still, it doesn't make any sense that he killed Jimmy."

The traffic had them slowed and there were plenty of opportunities to jump out of the car, but the guy in the back was too jumpy. Anything they did risked innocent bystanders.

"Why doesn't it make sense that he killed Jimmy?" Jordan asked.

"The guy who hired Jimmy didn't like violence. He was real angry when I shot up the coffee shop. We were supposed to pick up the lady and bring her to the cemetery, but we weren't supposed to hurt her. Then this guy goes and pops Jimmy."

Jordan didn't figure it was the violence that bothered the buyer. Most likely he didn't appreciate all the attention that resulted from the violence.

They came to the turnoff for the interstate, and Jordan tapped on the dash. "Lucy, take this turn here."

She frowned but did as he asked. Crossing town had slowed them down and given the agents an opportunity to catch up with them. The cemetery was at least twenty minutes away. More if he took the long way.

"Look," Jordan began. "We don't know who this guy is any more than you do, but we can help you. You were right about me. I have connections. We can protect you."

"I don't need help." His voice rose to a high-pitched squeal. "I need to know who this guy is so that I can take care of my own problem."

"Easy," Jordan soothed. "What's your name? You can tell me that at least. Just your first name."

"You can call me Jigsaw." He set down the gun and rubbed his face. "Everyone calls me that. I was good in wood shop."

"Okay, Jigsaw. I'm going to be honest with you. You're not going to fix this alone. I think you know that. That's why you came to us. You need our help."

"You gotta know who he is. What does he want from you?"

"That doesn't matter. It's not going to help

you find him." Jordan searched the traffic for any signs of a patrol car. He hoped they were smart enough to hang back. "What's with the cemetery? Why do you want to go back there?"

"We knocked out the cameras. I know how to get in and out of there without getting caught."

"Okay. Once we get there, what next?"

"You said you can help me." Jigsaw rested his hand on the gun. "How can you?"

"I work for the government. I have contacts."

"What kind of contacts?"

"I can help you disappear until this is all over."

"All right. All right." Sweat dripped from Jigsaw's temple. He jerked and rubbed his mouth. "What kind of deal can you offer me? I'm gonna need immunity or something like that."

"We can sort out the details later. First things first. You were hurt. How bad is it?"

"Not bad," Jigsaw replied, absently rubbing his leg. "But it's getting worse. I can't go to the hospital. They have to report that stuff. I think it's getting infected. I don't feel so good these days."

Jigsaw appeared to be running a fever, a sure sign the wound had gone septic.

Lucy glanced in the rearview mirror. "You need medical attention," she said softly. "You're tired. You've been fighting this thing on your own, but you don't have to. We both have the same enemy. We're not lying. We can help you."

Jordan rested his hand on her arm. "She's right, you know."

Ignoring the adrenaline spiking through his bloodstream, he forced a calm he didn't feel. Everything hinged on his ability to keep Jigsaw calm and talk him down from whatever plan he'd set in motion.

"Was Jimmy your friend?" Lucy asked, navigating traffic.

Though Jordan had declared a moratorium on the subject less than an hour before, he wanted to kiss her. Lucy's instincts were spot-on, and his admiration for her grew.

"Yeah." His eyes glassy, Jigsaw pinched the bridge of his nose and shook his head. "We grew up together. Went to school together. He had this idea that we could become security guys or something. But, like, for people like us. People on the other side of the law. But we had to make a name for ourselves first. And there was money, too."

They took the exit for the street fronting the cemetery, and Jordan caught sight of a familiar SUV behind them. Even though Jordan had done his best to slow them down, Karp must have run every stoplight to get here.

A black-and-white squad car turned off the main road, and Jordan's heart stalled. If Jigsaw thought he was walking into a trap, there was no telling what he might do.

Lucy jerked the wheel and pointed. "Is this the entrance you want me to use?"

The distraction worked. Jigsaw focused on the gate and missed the squad car completely. She slowed and followed the cemetery lane toward the chapel.

Jigsaw pressed his hand to his middle. "I don't feel so good."

"You're sick," Lucy said, her voice gentle. "Let us call an ambulance for you."

"How do I know this isn't a trap? How do I know you're playing straight?"

Lucy pulled before the chapel and placed the car in Park. "You don't. All you have is my word." She stretched around and held out her hand. "If you give me the gun, I promise I'll make sure you're put into hiding. You don't have to do this alone."

Jigsaw glanced at the gun on the seat but made no move to pick it up. "Tell him to get out."

"No." Jordan shook his head. "Absolutely not. There's no way I'm leaving her alone."

"It's all right," Lucy said, her attention focused on Jigsaw, her voice serene. "Just hand me the gun."

Jordan caught a flash of movement out of the corner of his eye. Jigsaw must have seen it, too, because he lunged for the gun. Lucy was closer, her hand already stretched across the seat.

The next instant, a gunshot exploded through the car.

FOURTEEN

Pressing her hands against her ears, Lucy staggered from the car. Arms encircled her, supporting her. Her ears were ringing, preventing her from hearing anything properly. She glanced behind her in time to see two policemen hauling Jigsaw from the scene. His feet dragged, but his mouth worked. He appeared to be hollering at the two officers. At least he was alive.

She hadn't shot him. They'd both lunged for the gun, and she wasn't certain which of them had reached it first. She remembered only the noise and a faint metallic smell.

Her knees buckled. Jordan scooped her into his arms and carried her to the stairs of the chapel. His gaze intense, he performed a brief, impersonal pat down.

"Are you hurt anywhere?" he demanded.

His voice sounded as though he was speaking underwater, and she realized it was her hearing that was the problem. Weary to the bone, she stared blankly into the distance.

"No." She rubbed the side of her head. "I can't—"

Jordan drew her against his chest. "The ringing will go away soon. You were too close when the gun went off."

The discomfort was already abating, and she could hear voices, though they were muffled and slightly distorted. Her stomach lurched, and she pressed two fingers against her mouth. Black spots danced in front of her eyes.

Jordan's heart beat a steady cadence against her ear, and she concentrated on the tempo. With an effort born of sheer will, she focused on her breathing, willing her lungs to move in and out. She fixated on the texture of Jordan's button-down shirt and the hint of cologne lingering in the material.

She didn't know how long they sat like that, but eventually her panic subsided, and her thoughts cleared. She fit perfectly against him. If she didn't know better, she'd have thought he was made for her. But that kind of thinking was dangerous. He didn't feel the same. Maybe she was better off this way. She wasn't the sort of person who craved a white-hot love that burned bright and then burned out.

The new beginnings of a relationship were always the most frightening—the uncertainty, the feeling of careening out of control. She much preferred when love settled into the comfort of a well-loved sweater, pilled and worn and comfortable. Jordan had made it clear that wasn't in their future.

The more time she spent with him, the more she worried that even their friendship was fragile and doomed. Because if they stayed friends, she'd have to cheer him through his life; she'd have to watch him fall in love with someone else. She'd have to feign indifference when his personal life moved on without her, and she didn't know if she had it in her.

More patrols arrived along with an ambulance. Lucy wasn't certain how much time passed, but as the minutes ticked by, she felt as though she was swimming toward the surface once more. The ringing in her ears gradually settled to a low-level buzz. The sun was too bright, but she'd left her sunglasses in the car, and it was currently the center of attention for the police.

With Jigsaw alive and on his way to the hospital, the scene was much more relaxed than the day Jimmy was killed.

The officers milled around, laughing and chatting. All traces of the harrowing incident had been swept away. Karp separated from a knot of officers and joined them.

He was dressed casually in jeans and a polo shirt and appeared more disheveled than she'd ever seen him. Two additional patrol cars had joined the scene.

"Was it him?" Karp directed the question to Jordan without preamble.

She felt Jordan's nod against her cheek. "Yeah. It's our guy."

"Looks like he'll be fine. The bullet only grazed him, but the wound's infected. They'll keep him in the hospital until the infection is cleared."

"Make sure they know he's a flight risk. He doesn't trust us."

"Can't say that I blame him after today," Karp said. "I was in the car when I got your call. I don't want to count the number of traffic laws I broke getting here. How did he get to you guys? Why did he come for you in the first place?"

"We went off-site for lunch," Jordan said. "And that's where he found us. He must have been watching the parking lot at Consolidated Unlimited."

Jordan filled in his colleague about the events of the past hour, and their voices droned over her. Too dazed by the encounter to move, Lucy waited for Jordan to pull away, but he didn't. If

Karp thought it odd that she was leaning heavily on Jordan, he gave no indication. Right then, she really didn't care what anyone thought.

"Okay," Karp said when Jordan finished his report. "I'll have Westover canvass the area. If someone is looking for Jigsaw, let's pull that thread. I want to know everyone he's been in contact with since his buddy's death. If Jigsaw knows there's a hit out on him, then somebody else knows something."

"Agreed."

As the two men discussed their plan of action going forward, a gray Chevy Impala drove into the parking lot.

A man Lucy recognized as Detective Ryan unfolded from the car and approached them. "You two are like a couple of bad pennies. You gotta stop hanging out in the cemetery. I got most of the story on the way over, so we can save the recap. Only thing I can't figure out is why he dragged you guys back to the scene of the crime."

Jordan grunted. "Near as I can tell, Jigsaw felt guilty about doing a runner when Jimmy got shot. It was like he was compelled to come back here. It must have made a weird sort of sense to him. The cemetery is isolated, not exactly a hotbed of activity. They'd scoped the place already. He knew which cameras were out of commission. I honestly think he was hurt and confused. I don't think he had an endgame in mind beyond finding out who killed Jimmy and put a hit on him."

"Makes sense," Karp said. "After talking to known associates of the pair, Jimmy was the leader." He studied them closer. "You two all right?"

Her head was splitting, but Lucy swallowed hard and nodded. "I'm fine. I thought I shot him. We both went for the gun…"

She relived the scene in her mind, the gunshot and the sudden silence, and the panicky fear built inside her once more.

Jordan framed her face between his hands and stared intently into her eyes, his own burning. Her heart turned at the concern she saw there.

"It's over," he said. "He's gone, and he's not coming back."

They both knew the danger was far from resolved, but it was enough for now.

Detective Ryan stared at the cluster of officers near Lucy's car. "I don't want to draw any more attention to Jigsaw than we have to. As far as anyone knows, this guy is still on the run. Let's keep it that way for as long as we can. When I need a statement, I'll call you down to the station. For now, why don't the two of you clear out."

Lucy sat up with a gasp. "Work! We should have been back an hour ago. Sue is going to be worried sick."

"Don't worry," Jordan said. "I'll tell them we were in a minor fender bender or something. It's close enough to the truth."

Lucy hung her head and clutched her pounding skull with both hands. "I need an aspirin."

Jordan stood and pulled her to her feet. "C'mon. Let's get you home. We're taking the rest of the day off."

Karp handed Jordan the keys to his car. Lucy didn't know how he planned on getting home himself, and at that moment she was too exhausted to care.

The trip back to her house was a silent one. She barely remembered the passing scenery. Once they arrived, she made her way wearily into the house and collapsed on the sofa.

Jordan took the chair across from her. "Are you sure you're okay?"

"I almost feel sorry for Jigsaw."

"Don't." Jordan stood, his hands on his hips. "He and Jimmy made the choice to put themselves in that situation. They weren't collecting Christmas presents for orphans—they were hired to kidnap you. Save your sympathy for the people who are worthy of it."

Pressure built behind her eyes and she leaned forward, willing herself to stay strong.

The sofa depressed beside her, and Jordan wrapped his arm around her shoulder. "Oh, Lucy. It's all right. You can cry."

His words released a surge of emotion, and she moved toward him, sobbing against his shirt. He held her like that for a long time. He didn't say anything, just let her cry, and for that she was grateful. Feeling truly safe at last, Lucy burrowed into the security of his warm embrace.

After a long while, she hiccuped. "I was distracted when I left the restaurant. I should have seen him in the car. I didn't even notice."

Jordan rocked her back and forth, his hands moving in soothing circles over her shoulders. "You can't do that to yourself. I've been through more than my fair share of what-ifs, and they'll destroy you if you let them."

Lifting her watery gaze to his, she blinked. "I'm sorry. I'm not usually a crier. I don't know what's wrong with me."

He wiped the tears from her cheeks with the pads of his thumbs. "You've been through a lot. I think you've earned it."

All words deserted her. There was no way to

tell him that she wasn't crying over what she'd been through, though the events of the past few weeks had weakened her. She was mourning another lost opportunity for happiness. She wanted a chance at a future together, and the longing was so intense, it hurt. She couldn't remember wanting something so bad and knowing how impossible that was.

When the time came, she'd give him permission to turn his back on her. She'd give him permission to relinquish whatever debt he felt he owed Brandt. She'd deny her own heartache.

Because the way she felt now, there was no way they were ever going to be friends after this was all over.

Jordan glanced out the window of the rented house and straight into Lucy's sunroom. She'd closed the curtains, but he could picture the exact placement of her guinea pig cage and the fringed floor lamp near the table.

He'd nearly slipped into dangerous territory today, but he'd pulled himself back from the brink before he made a colossal mistake.

He'd done the right thing. When Brandt had asked him to look out for Lucy, Jordan was fairly certain he hadn't meant in the romantic sense. Circumstances had them both running on high emotion. She was frightened, and Jordan was a connection to someone she'd loved and lost.

She was transferring her feelings or something like that. He wasn't entirely certain of all the psychological terms. What she felt for him was only a reflection of his friendship with Brandt. If he and Lucy took their relationship further, sooner or later she was going to realize her mistake, and then he'd lose her for good. He'd rather have her friendship than nothing at all.

The phone rang, and he recognized the number as belonging to a buddy of his who worked at the embassy in Islamabad.

Jordan picked up the call. "What's up, Mike?"

The two exchanged a few pleasantries before Mike got down to the reason for his call. "I finally got a chance to visit that jeweler you mentioned. I asked him about the ring."

Jordan's pulse spiked. "What did he have to say?"

"Not much. Mostly what we suspected already. Brandt gave him a photo and asked him to make an exact replica."

"Did he know why?"

"Brandt told the jeweler the same thing he told you. He wanted to propose to his fiancée properly."

Brandt's fiancée. *Lucy.* Jordan went hot

and cold at the same time. The reminder was timely—and sobering.

"Did the jeweler know if Brandt specifically mentioned Lucy's name?" Jordan asked.

He needed to know if the ring was for Lucy. He needed to know if the man he'd risked his life for, the man he'd nearly died with, was the same man he thought he knew in his heart.

"Nope. Nobody mentioned a name. All I got was *his fiancée.* So either the jeweler didn't know her name, or he doesn't remember it."

Frustration rode Jordan. He couldn't avoid speaking to Lucy any longer. She might have an answer for the duplicate engagement ring. And if she didn't, that was a chance he had to take. He flashed back to their lunch this afternoon. Come to think of it, she hadn't been wearing the ring.

Jordan pinched the bridge of his nose. "Anything else?"

"Yeah." A heavy pause followed Mike's admission. "There's something else. The jeweler remembers Brandt being in the shop with someone else. A woman."

Jordan's chest tightened. "What did she look like?"

"She wasn't wearing a hijab, but he got the feeling she was local. Dark hair. Pretty. Maybe five-four or five-five. That's about all I could get out of him."

The band around Jordan's chest squeezed even tighter. There wasn't enough detail to identify her. He might have been more frustrated if it weren't for the fact that he'd seen Brandt with a woman who matched the description the night before the bombing.

"Okay," Jordan said. "Anything else?"

Right now, all they had was conjecture. He knew better than to assemble a puzzle before he had all the pieces. How could he spend that much time with someone and not see the signs? He was trained to spot deception. He wasn't going to believe anything false about Brandt until he had solid proof.

"Yeah, this is where things get really weird." Though they were on a secure line, Mike pitched his voice low. "After I started asking questions, I got a visit from a couple of CIA guys. You know the ones. They came by the embassy a few times. Always wearing sunglasses. One old, one young, one pale, one—"

"Yeah. I know the two." Pakistan was crawling with American intelligence officers. While their work often overlapped, each agency held jurisdiction over their individual cases and was responsible for different areas of intelligence. "What did they want?"

"Near as I can tell, they wanted to know if I was on the take, if I was being bribed."

"Wait—what?" Jordan sputtered.

"Yeah. Took me a while to figure it out. They kept talking about the jewelry shop and how far the American dollar goes in Pakistan. When they finally got around to asking me why I was at the shop, they got all squirrelly." Mike's heavy sigh circled halfway around the globe. "After they left, I did a little digging. That shop has been on their radar for months. The CIA has been investigating foreign officials for bribery and the jeweler is the go-between."

"Wait a second. You're saying someone in the jewelry shop is brokering the bribes?"

"Yep. You know how it works. Say a Chinese company wants a copper mine in an area controlled by insurgents. Someone from the company buys a ring worth four thousand dollars. Only they pay twenty, and suddenly the insurgents in the area go underground. The copper mine is green-lighted. Do you follow?"

On a hunch, Jordan asked, "What about drones? Have you heard anything about a market for drone technology?"

With a few bribes and the proper drone technology, foreign businesses effectively sidestepped American security, putting everyone in danger. Insurgents weren't exactly known for keeping their promises. Dealing with them was a risky and often deadly business.

"I don't think so. No…wait. Maybe. There was something last year. Apparently, the insurgents are looking to buy technology. I didn't hear anything about drones specifically. More like infrastructure. Communications. That sort of thing. They want to cause trouble from the inside. You remember when the power grid went down in South America?"

"Yeah," Jordan replied, knowing he was on the edge of something significant.

"Apparently, that got a lot of attention around here," Mike continued. "According to the scuttlebutt, there's talk that insurgent groups are changing tactics. Less shock and awe and more sabotage from the inside. There's opportunity in chaos."

"When did you first start hearing those rumors? How long has it been out there?"

Jordan had to see this through, no matter what answers he discovered. It was the right thing to do. Why, then, did it feel so wrong?

A great pressure settled on his chest.

"Oh, that's old news," Mike said, oblivious to the chain of events his words had set in motion. "That's why I kind of forgot about it. I think it's been at least a year since I heard there was a market for hacking over here. Haven't heard anything lately. It's not in the security briefings."

"Or maybe they aren't looking because they already found what they want."

The ring. The woman he'd seen with Brandt. The jeweler.

Jordan didn't want to believe that Brandt had deliberately put Lucy in danger. The evidence was damning, but it wasn't proof. The timing didn't fit, either. Brandt had been gone over a year. Then again, who knew how long the plan to impersonate Lucy had been in place. Maybe someone had tried before, only they hadn't been caught until now.

Mike chuckled. "When those guys from the CIA saw me walk into the shop asking about a ring, they thought they had an American on the hook for bribery. Good thing I pay my mortgage on time. They're probably poring over my financial records with a fine-tooth comb. Which means they're watching anybody who enters that shop for obvious reasons." He cleared his throat. "Look, I'm sorry. We both know what this means."

Jordan needed to keep a clear head. He had to consider all the possibilities. Brandt may have been unaware of the purpose of the jewelry shop he'd chosen to duplicate the ring, or he may have stumbled onto more than he was expecting.

And there was another option they had to consider. Someone had been tipped off about the surveillance equipment. Someone had known where to find Jordan and Brandt. Maybe Jordan's survival wasn't such a fortunate break, after all. Not if Brandt had been the true target all along.

"I know what this means." Jordan's vision fractured around the edges. "There's a chance Brandt was on the take."

FIFTEEN

Lucy stared at her screen, the code blurring. Shoving back from her desk, she pressed her knuckles against her eyes until she saw stars. She'd been going at this all day, and she was no closer to a solution. For the past week, her concentration had been shot.

She had to get out of here. Maybe take a walk or something. She was reaching for her purse when her coworker Vance Eagan rounded the corner.

He was short and balding with black-rimmed glasses and a slight paunch. He'd been dating Emily Franklin, one of the coders on the floor, for the past year. He never missed an opportunity to walk past Emily's desk during the workday.

"Hey, Lucy," Vance said, leaning against her cubicle. "You talk to that new guy on the Greenspace project yet?"

"Jordan?"

"Yeah. That's the guy. Alan can't stop singing his praises. You think he might consider taking a look at the stopgap measures on the new rollout?"

"I can ask."

Vance's shoulders sagged. "That'd be great. I've been taking a lot of heat over the past few weeks. This thing is driving me crazy. I could use a new set of eyes."

Lucy dug into her purse for her keys. Maybe she'd go for a drive, instead. Anything to get away from this building for a while.

Now that Jigsaw was safely in custody, the threat had abated. There'd been no contact with the buyer, either. They were certainly no closer to discovering the identity of her doppelgänger, and she was stalled out and frustrated.

Because of the security concerns, she'd been shuttling between work and home and nowhere else, and she was going stir-crazy. She feared if she asked Jordan, he'd refuse. Maybe it was better to beg forgiveness than ask permission. What were the chances of being carjacked twice, anyway?

She set down her keys with a sigh. Better to be frustrated and alive than distracted and dead.

"Is the project behind schedule?" she asked, dimly aware that Vance had said something else. "I can take a look at it if you want."

"That's okay. I know you're behind on your own work."

She'd taken so many days off this past month, she was drowning in code. Not to mention she'd had her mind on other things. Her work was suffering. This morning had been a bust.

She hadn't realized the rest of the staff had noticed. "Well, I'll let Jordan know you could use his help, anyway. He's in a meeting with the rest of the Greenspace team."

"Thanks. I could really use a win on this one." Vance's ruddy complexion darkened. "You remember that security breach we had a few weeks ago?"

Her hands stilled on her purse. "Yeah. I remember. What about it?"

"Apparently, my computer was involved." He looked away and scuffed the floor. "I had my password written on the back of the keyboard."

"Oh, Vance." Lucy shook her head. "You know better."

"I know. But it seems like they make us change that stupid password every other day. I kept forgetting it, and IT was getting annoyed. I just wrote it down. We work in a secure building. I didn't figure it was a big deal. How did someone from outside get in here in the first place? That's not my fault."

Lucy feigned nonchalance. "Did anyone else

know that's where you kept your password? Did anyone else ever work on your computer?"

"No one works on my computer, as far as I know." He lifted one shoulder in a careless shrug. "But they don't exactly give us a lot of privacy around here. Anybody could have seen me flip over my keyboard. I guess maybe Sheila might have noticed. She sits across the aisle. And maybe Emily."

Since the company already knew Vance's computer was involved, Lucy doubted there was anything new to learn. Still, she'd keep the information in the back of her mind for future reference.

"That's a bummer," she said. "They're still really jumpy upstairs because of that security breach. Did they try anyone else's computer?"

She already knew the answer, but there was no harm in asking.

"They rifled through half of the desks before they got to mine. It's like those thieves who go through neighborhoods looking for unlocked cars. I was the only stupid one. Now I feel like I gotta look over my shoulder all the time."

"We all make mistakes, Vance. You can't beat yourself up."

And he didn't even know the half of it. No one in the company aside from a few key players knew the hacker had tried to frame Lucy. She'd prefer to keep it that way as long as possible.

Vance harrumphed. "It's rotten luck. I'm up for a promotion this year. How's it going to look when my review comes up?"

Maybe it *was* just a coincidence that someone had discovered his password. Neither Sheila nor Emily struck Lucy as the type to do something like this. Especially Emily. She was taller than average and painfully shy. Everyone in the company had been pleased when she and Vance began dating.

"I'm sorry they're giving you a hard time," Lucy said.

"Not hard, exactly. I just feel like everyone is looking at me all of a sudden." He glanced over his shoulder. "I feel like I'm under surveillance. The whole company has been paranoid. Frank even gave Emily the third degree this morning because she didn't register her new car with Security."

"Wait." Lucy's attention sharpened. "Emily bought a new car?"

"Yeah. One of those hybrid things. It's crazy cool. Practically drives itself."

The fine hairs on the back of her neck stirred. "A new car is expensive."

"You're telling me. Too rich for my blood."

Lucy forced a chuckle. "Did a rich uncle die or something?"

"You must be psychic," Vance said. "Only it was her aunt who died and left her some money. Now she wants to go to Cancún over the winter, but I can't afford the airfare. She offered to pay my way, but that feels even worse." Vance shuddered. "Like I'm a kept man or something."

"C'mon." Lucy stifled a smile. "I'm sure she was only trying to be nice."

"I know. You're right." He straightened his tie. "Look, let me know if you think Jordan can help out on this thing. Like I said, I could really use a win. Might make up for what happened."

"I'll ask him. I promise. Just as soon as he gets back."

She'd also tell him about Emily's new car. The whole "rich aunt dying" seemed a little too convenient considering what had been happening around here lately.

Vance had only been gone a moment when Sue peered over the partition. "Psst, Lucy. I almost forgot. Someone left this on my desk, but I think it was supposed to go to you."

A padded manila envelope dropped over the wall.

It was postmarked the day before and had no return address. Lucy ripped open the envelope and discovered a key and a slip of paper.

Unfolding the letter revealed a number and the name of a bank. Nothing else. No signature. No instructions.

Studying the items further, she noted the number on the piece of paper matched an etched number on the key. Nothing else indicated what she was supposed to do.

Lucy shot to her feet and circled around to Sue's desk. "Did you see who left this?"

"The mail room. They must have mixed up our desks."

"Oh." Lucy didn't bother hiding her disappointment. "Okay."

Of course it had come in the mail. If this was from the buyer, he wasn't going to waltz in here and drop an envelope on her desk in plain view of everyone. The place was carpeted with cameras.

Sue frowned. "Are you all right?"

"Yeah. It's nothing."

Returning to her desk, Lucy dropped the envelope and considered the contents. She'd probably ruined whatever evidence they might have discovered. In the hope of saving any fingerprints that might be left, she lifted the corner with her pencil and placed the envelope in a file folder.

She glanced over her shoulder and huffed. Jordan's seat was still empty. He'd been in the meeting all morning. Considering he was here undercover, he'd become an invaluable part of the team in a remarkably short amount of time. Alan was going to weep real tears when he left. Especially if the Greenspace project was ongoing.

Meeting or no meeting, she had to talk to Jordan. Thankfully, by the time she got to the conference room, everyone was standing. Shifting from foot to foot and clutching the file folder, she waited impatiently while the employees gathered their belongings and offered their postmortems on the presentation they'd just watched.

Jordan was one of the last people to exit the room.

She caught his arm and pulled him back inside. "I think he's made contact."

After studying the key and the note, his expression turned grim. "It's a safe-deposit box. I'll check it out."

"I'm going with you."

It wasn't like she was being terribly productive anyway.

Jordan was reluctant but offered only token resistance. He drove and they arrived a scant fifteen minutes later. The bank was located downtown, and they parked in an underground garage. Once inside the cavernous lobby, Lucy gave her name and the box number to an attendant, who ushered them into a vault. Lucy's heels clicked sharply on the tile floor. The walls of the vault were lined from floor to ceiling with safe-deposit boxes of varying sizes.

The woman turned her key in the lock before leaving them alone.

Lucy reached for the metal square, but Jordan placed his hand on her arm. "Let me take a look."

He pulled the box gently from its shelf and lifted the metal cover. Inside was a cell phone, along with a smaller brown envelope.

He opened the flap and dumped the contents onto his outstretched palm.

Two sparkling diamonds glittered beneath the artificial light.

Lucy gasped. "I'm no gemstone expert, but those are at least a carat or more."

"At least," Jordan replied grimly.

"A payment?"

"Looks like it. Untraceable. Easy to transport overseas."

She tipped back her head. "Can we pull the security cameras? See who rented the safe-deposit box?"

"I'll have Karp request the warrants this afternoon, but I doubt it'll do us any good. Chances are, he sent someone else to rent the box, and I doubt they used a real name and address."

Lucy turned on the phone. There was one number programmed into the contacts, without any other information, and one message in the text box: Can you deliver? Along with a date that marked a week from Wednesday.

They all had agreed the buyer was looking for the secure uplink codes. He wanted to control the drones at the source, where his connection would be untraceable. Clearly he had rudimentary knowledge of how the system worked.

An idea took shape in Lucy's mind.

Rudimentary knowledge was not genuine understanding, and that would be the buyer's undoing. Adrenaline rushed through her system.

She turned to Jordan. "Do you trust me?"

Without hesitation he replied, "Yes."

"Good. Because I know what to do."

She typed: Yes. But this time, you follow my instructions.

This was a side of Lucy that Jordan hadn't seen before now.

She stood at the head of the conference room, poised and passionate. While the rest of the team wasn't convinced of her solution, they were coming around.

Brushing the platinum hair from her forehead, she pointed at the screen. "We already know this guy is smart enough to recognize implanted malware and corrupted code. That means we have to give him the pure code."

Westover coughed and fidgeted in his chair. "And then just let him take over control of our drones? Doesn't that defeat the purpose?"

"No." She flipped to the next screen. "We reprogram the drones."

After hearing her plan, Jordan had convinced the commander of the drone program to fly in for the meeting. His gray hair was cropped short and his weathered face indicated a long and eventful career. He'd worn his dress blues and the rows of medals on his chest were impressive. His buy-in was the most important part of the plan.

Too bad he didn't look convinced. "Reprogramming the drones would take months," he scoffed.

"Not if we rely on the code that's already embedded." Lucy advanced the screen. "I worked it out last night. The drones are already programmed to record the ID of their controllers. We simply add a line to relay that information back to the mainframe. Then we program the mainframe to alert headquarters if one of the drones is being operated from an unrecognized location."

"Okay, okay." The commander ducked his head and scribbled on a pad of paper. Everyone remained silent while he worked out the problem. "I see where you're going with this, but it still won't work. Even if we have a pinpoint location for the source, it could take us an hour or more to reach that location. Which means by the time we figure out where this guy is, he's liable to drop a missile on our embassy. I can't take the risk."

"I've taken that into account, as well." Lucy's eyes glittered with excitement. "The delay is actually beneficial. All drones are equipped with safety protocols prior to rollout. That way, if anything goes wrong during the testing phase, we can remotely kill the sequence. Here's the thing. We don't remove that code when the drone goes live, because that's inefficient. Instead, we simply build in a switch. We shut off the feature. I'm recommending that we reinstate the safety feature. It's a little more complicated than, say, flipping a switch. But it's a shockingly simple line of code."

Karp leaned forward. "This could work. We give him the pure code, and then we wait for him to activate the drone. We'll have his location and a fail-safe on the drone."

The commander clasped his hands. "I'm still worried about the timing. We have a really small window between when he activates the drone and when we scramble a team to locate him."

"That's true, but we have an advantage. We believe he's local. The one IP address we were able to identify was pinpointed to a library not three miles from where we're standing."

"Okay, but this guy will know something's up when he goes to deploy a missile and nothing happens. Even if he's next door, if he rabbits too quickly, we could lose him."

"That's where we rely on human nature," Lucy declared triumphantly, as though she'd been building to this crescendo the whole time. "This guy doesn't trust us. We've already tried to double-cross him by giving him code infected with malware. So what do you do when you're not sure if what you have is trustworthy?"

Dawning understanding washed over Jordan. "You test it."

"Yes." Lucy pointed at him. "You test it. We're only dealing with the buyer. He isn't going to start out by dropping a bomb. He won't risk it. He's going to do something innocuous, like maybe go for a joyride or take a few pictures. That's when we pinpoint his location. Because, chances are, he's going to make certain nothing goes wrong before he puts this code up for a bidding war. That's when we get him. If he tries to fire up the drone a second time for the highest bidder, we'll already have a team in place to capture him and a fail-safe on the drone."

For a moment, everyone in the room sat in stunned silence.

Then Karp let out a whoop.

Shocked by the uncharacteristic display of emotion, they all turned.

Karp pumped his fists. "This could work. It's simple. It's elegant. It's as foolproof as we're ever going to get."

"It's genius." Westover shook his head with a dazed grin. "It's absolute genius."

Lucy glowed beneath their praise. "Thank you. It's really quite logical. I can't believe we didn't think of it sooner."

Jordan's heart thudded in his chest. She was stunning. There was no way to unravel even a tenth of the emotion she stirred inside him. He was attracted to her looks, but he was absolutely staggered by her intelligence. There was nothing more seductive than confidence, and Lucy was glowing.

"Okay, okay." Karp held up his arms. "Let's settle down. How do we transfer the code? I'm not risking another dead drop. He doesn't trust us, and I don't trust him."

"That's even easier," Lucy said. "We set up an email account and give him the password. I attach the code to an email and save it in the drafts folder. That way, he can access the drafts folder without giving away his location. As long as the email is never actually sent, there's no tracking information. Hackers use the same method to exchange illegal code all the time. It's practically foolproof."

Westover pressed the heel of his hand against his eyes. "Then why didn't we do that before?"

"Because we were playing by his rules. I think he suspected that something was off, and that's why he wanted to meet in person. You were right—the meeting in the park was a test. Judging by the diamonds, we passed the test. He didn't blame us for the lost flash drive—he blamed his own couriers. This time we're in charge, and we set the rules."

Westover elbowed Jordan in the side. "Looks like you'll be going home soon. Back to Maryland."

A flash of panic temporarily blinded Jordan. "I'm finishing up the communications project. I've got a few more months on base."

"Didn't you watch the news this morning? A British tanker was seized on its way through the Strait of Hormuz. You mark my words—we'll all be scrambled by next week."

Jordan glanced at Lucy. She was speaking to the commander of drone operations, a wide grin on her face. She returned to her seat, and the commander stood and moved to her place to address the room.

"I'm giving this plan the green light," he declared with enough pomp to make it appear that he'd solved the problem single-handedly. "I'll have the code changed and alert my crews to the plan. We have until next Wednesday according to the timeline from the buyer, and that won't be a problem. After that, it's a waiting game."

"We won't have to wait long," Karp said. "I've been tracking this guy for two years. When he moves, he moves quickly."

"What about Lucy?" Westover asked. "Where does she fit into all this?"

"Well." Karp raised his bushy eyebrows. "She should act like a woman who's just been given a couple of diamonds that are worth about ten thousand dollars apiece. As far as our buyer knows, Jordan is her boyfriend. They need to look like they're celebrating a windfall. Maybe a fancy dinner out on the town. A shopping spree. Talk of a European vacation over dinner. Consider a trip to a car lot. Let's make it appear as though she's considering some big-ticket items."

Everyone looked at the two of them, and Jordan nodded his approval. "Sounds good. I'll set something up."

Lucy smiled at him, and in that moment he understood why they called it "falling" in love. When she looked at him like that, his heart tumbled head over heels. Westover congratulated her, and she turned the same radiant smile on him.

Jordan's mood came crashing down. She'd given him every opportunity to pursue a relationship, and he'd rebuffed her at every turn. With quiet dignity, she'd accepted his refusal.

If everything went according to plan, he could be back in the field by the end of the month. He wouldn't be seeing Lucy on a day-to-day basis anymore. They wouldn't be carpooling to work or having dinner in the evenings. He wouldn't have to fight his feelings any longer. She'd be safe, and he'd be on the other side of the world.

She wouldn't turn to him with a smile meant just for him or lean in close for a comment only for his ears. She was young and vibrant, and she had her whole future ahead of her. Her life had been on hold while she'd mourned, and he was watching her awaken.

To all things a season. It was time for him to move on. She deserved someone who wouldn't be a perpetual reminder of the sorrow that had been her constant companion this past year.

He'd done the right thing.

Why, then, did he feel as though he'd just lost everything?

SIXTEEN

For her "date" with Jordan, Lucy wore a dress she'd bought for a friend's wedding the previous year. The floral pastel pattern was soft and feminine, and the belted waist showed off her figure to its best advantage. She'd paired the outfit with a pair of strappy pink sandals that made her feel tall. She'd received loads of compliments the last time she'd worn the outfit.

Not that this was a real date.

The team was feeling secure because the code had been delivered to the draft box of the dummy email account. Everything was going according to plan, and now it was time to act as though she was doing a victory lap.

In an abundance of caution, they'd been careful not to speak about where they were going ahead of time, and Jordan had arranged for a second team to follow them as extra backup.

He greeted her at the door wearing jeans, a button-up shirt and a tweed jacket. He must have splashed some cologne on his cheeks. As the scent drifted over her, her heart did that unwelcome rat-a-tat-tat.

She took a firm grip on her emotions. He was a friend. Nothing more. And this time she wasn't going to ruin things. She sensed his reluctance had something to do with loyalty to his friend, and though she didn't agree, she respected his decision.

In case the restaurant was cold, Lucy grabbed a sweater she'd draped over the chair.

Ever the gentleman, Jordan opened her car door. She'd miss these small displays of gallantry, but she was resigned to the parameters of their relationship.

As they drove downtown, he said, "One of the guys at work suggested a place in the Old Market—the Silver Feather. Have you been there?"

Lucy gaped. "No. It's far too fancy for my budget. I knew we were celebrating, but I didn't know we were *celebrating*."

"Don't worry." Jordan grinned. "We'll expense it. This is all a part of the charade, after all."

His declaration did nothing to diminish her determination to enjoy the evening. For her own sanity, she'd made the decision to end their friendship after this was all over. She didn't trust herself around him, and she'd decided that going cold turkey was the best option. Staying in touch meant opening herself to more heartache.

She was treating this as something of a farewell supper. She didn't regret their time together, and she wanted a few more good memories to carry with her.

The Old Market area was located by the river. The sturdy turn-of-the-century warehouses along the waterfront had been converted into apartments, shops and restaurants. The city maintained the brick streets from the Depression-era work projects of the thirties, giving the area a timeless romantic appeal. Horse-drawn carriages made lazy circles in front of the shops, their hooves clip-clopping over the cobblestone-like streets.

The evening was beautiful, and the weather was temperate as they took a seat on the patio that abutted the sidewalk. Jordan couldn't have chosen a more romantic setting. A string of miniature Edison bulbs crisscrossed above them. They chatted about everything and nothing and watched as people strolled past them. There were couples holding hands and families pushing strollers. There were rowdy teenagers and solitary people with their heads bent over their phones as they walked.

The dinner was superb. The head chef even came to their table and chatted for a few minutes. Dessert was a decadent concoction featuring a chocolate globe that melted away when warm berry syrup was poured over the top to reveal a sumptuous opera cake inside.

After they'd eaten, Lucy leaned back in her chair. "I could get used to this."

She was stuffed and drowsy and wonderfully content.

"Me, too," Jordan declared, his tone capturing a hint of the melancholy she was feeling.

The sun dipped low on the horizon, and a stunning sunset streaked across the sky.

At times like this, everything seemed possible again, and her hope returned like a potent and heady drug. She'd been marking time for the past year, afraid to move forward, afraid to plan for the future. She'd been on a path with someone and that path had ended abruptly.

When Brandt died, her hopes and dreams for their future together had died with him. Now it was time for new hopes and new dreams. For too long fear had driven her actions. She'd feared putting her faith in something new because she feared losing everything. No more. She'd rather have joy in her life than live as a coward, afraid of loving because she was afraid of losing. She was ready to feel the happiness as well as the pain in her life.

Lost in their thoughts, they lingered over their

coffee, reluctant to break the contented bubble that had formed around them.

After several minutes, Jordan stood and reached for her hand. "Would you like to take a walk?"

She nodded and slipped her fingers into his. His hand was so large, yet hers seemed to fit perfectly.

The sun lingered on the horizon, bathing them in a twilight glow. The spring weather had brought crowds of people to the area, and they jostled for position on the wide sidewalks.

"I used to come down here all the time as a kid," Lucy said, then pointed. "There was an arcade right there."

"You're too young for arcades."

"It was retro."

She took him to an elaborate candy shop featuring row upon row of nostalgic candy. She picked out a sleeve of candy buttons and some Dubble Bubble gum.

"What are you getting?" she asked.

"Circus peanuts." He held up a bag of orange-colored candy. "I didn't know they still made these."

"They shouldn't!" She made a face. "They're gross."

"And your candy buttons aren't any less weird?"

"Touché." She unwrapped her gum. "Here's

something you don't know about me. I once won a bubble-blowing contest."

Though a little rusty, she managed to produce an enormous bubble. Using her index finger, she popped it before it splattered against her face.

"Ta-da."

"Very impressive. Your mother must have been proud."

"Bubble blowing was not considered a source of pride in our household," Lucy mused, tangled in a memory. "I always had gum in my hair. Drove my mom absolutely crazy. I had this long blond hair, and she'd have to cut out chunks."

"No one should exit childhood without having at least one wad of gum stuck in their hair. It's a rite of passage."

They crossed the street and she caught sight of her favorite ice-cream shop. Snatching Jordan's hand, she dragged him down the sidewalk. There was nothing wrong with leaving him a few memories. This city had been her home for her whole life, but she was ready to make a change.

Her experiences over the past few weeks had been terrifying, but they'd also revealed a source of inner strength. She was ready to face bigger challenges and take bigger risks.

"You're going to love this place," she said,

tugging Jordan along. "They make bubble gum ice cream."

His expression was skeptical. "I'm not really hungry, and I don't know how I feel about bubble gum ice cream."

"It's the best, but don't worry. They have other flavors."

The place was packed, but the line moved quickly. A baby in the stroller ahead of them made faces, entertaining them while they waited. On the advice of the server, Jordan chose a honey-cake-flavored ice cream while Lucy continued her bubble gum–themed evening.

They perched on a low stone wall and Lucy sighed. "This is like eating a memory."

Jordan laughed. "That's very descriptive. Did you come here with your family?"

"My mom. My dad left when I was little."

"I'm sorry. That must have been hard."

"It's all right. I don't really remember his time with us much. My mom isn't easy to get along with. He lives in California. I see him every couple of years. We send Christmas cards. I have a half brother. You know how it is."

"Blended families have their challenges."

"We're not blended so much as an extension of each other. I wasn't the only kid at school being raised by a single parent. It just seemed normal." She stared at her melting ice cream.

"Even so, I wanted something different for my kids. I *want* something different for my kids," she corrected.

It was time to start dreaming of a future again.

"Brandt would have made a good father."

"Yes." She stood and tossed her unfinished ice cream into the trash. "He would have."

For some reason, his words left her angry. Brandt would have made a good father. He'd have made a good husband. She'd been living the past year on all the things that might have been, and she was ready to let go of the pain.

She missed him—she'd always miss him—but she refused to live her life in a state of suspended animation, and Jordan made her feel guilty for moving on.

He caught her arm. "I'm sorry, Lucy. I didn't mean to upset you."

"I'm not upset. I'm tired. I'm tired of being sad. I'm tired of being lonely. I want to look forward to the future instead of thinking of all the things that might have been. I'm ready to be happy again."

"Then what's stopping you?"

You, she wanted to shout.

That wasn't fair. She pressed the heels of her hands against her temples. None of this was Jordan's fault. Having a connection to Brandt had brought her peace this past month. It wasn't his fault she'd started to fall in love with him.

Why couldn't he be old and mean and ugly?

Why did he have to be the only other person who had ever made her heart pound and her breath catch?

Lucy clutched her cross-body bag against her hip. "Nothing. Nothing is stopping me."

Her head down, she plunged into the crowd. What was wrong with her? There was no point in blaming Jordan because he didn't return her feelings.

"Lucy, wait!" Jordan called.

Feeling rebellious, she picked up her pace. She caught sight of Westover trailing them in the SUV. It wasn't as though she was alone. She was never alone lately. There was always someone watching and listening.

The sidewalks were crowded, and she made her way toward a coffee shop on the corner. She missed being autonomous. Lately she had people listening to her, watching her and following her all the time. All she wanted was some peace and quiet. Maybe that was why she was out of sorts. She needed a little time *alone* for once.

To her continued annoyance, the coffee shop was packed, as well. The outside patio was crowded with people laughing and talking together. The evening was too beautiful to sit hunched over a computer, although at least one person had chosen just that.

Her feet hurt and she wished she hadn't worn these stupid shoes. Her eyes burned.

Her phone buzzed and she stared at the screen.

For a minute she hoped it was Jordan, but it was Sue reminding her of the baby shower they were supposed to attend for another coworker, and she mentally berated herself.

Her heart simply refused to listen to all her self-talk.

She glanced up just as a man on a bike came careening down the sidewalk. The woman in front of her leaped out of the way. As Lucy lunged to the side, her heel slipped into a crack in the pavement. Her phone went flying.

She pitched sideways, though her foot remained stuck, and bumped into a chair, causing a domino effect. A man jumped up and the flimsy table overturned, tossing a woman's laptop to the ground. The screen shattered and the woman yelped.

Lucy's foot slipped free of her strappy sandal, and she flew backward.

Jordan managed to grab Lucy a split second before her head hit the pavement.

He clutched her against his frantically beating heart. "Are you all right?"

No matter how much he tried to avoid it, she kept landing in his arms. Why did God insist on thrusting temptation into his path?

"I'm fine," Lucy said, stirring against him. "Just clumsy."

A well-dressed middle-aged woman approached them. "I think this is your shoe."

Lucy accepted the sandal. "Thanks."

A young man extended his hand. "Your phone, miss."

The screen was cracked, though not as bad as before. She was going to go broke replacing phones at this rate. The woman from the coffee shop retrieved her shattered laptop and glared in the direction the bike had taken.

When it became clear there were no serious injuries, tables were righted, and nervous laughter abounded.

Westover joined them, his chest rising and falling with his rapid breathing. "I chased the guy down and caught up with him about a block away. I thought maybe the accident was deliberate, but he's clearly inebriated."

Lucy replaced her shoe, then smoothed her hair. "I'm fine. Just a little shaken up."

Westover glanced around, then lowered his voice. "I better skedaddle, just in case someone is watching."

"I'm ready to go home now," Lucy declared.

"I want to be in the car. At least I know no one is watching or listening to me there."

With one hand on the small of her back and his attention sharp, Jordan guided her to their parked car. Once they were safely inside, he vacillated between his duty and his loyalty. Despite the reckless biker who'd plowed down the sidewalk, the evening with Lucy had been wonderful.

The more he thought about the ring he'd discovered in Brandt's belongings, the more he realized he had no choice other than to speak with Lucy. He was running out of time to gather answers. Though she'd been through a harrowing ordeal these past couple of weeks, his questions could no longer wait.

No matter where the answers led, he had to know the truth, and the car was the best place to have the conversation.

Keeping one hand on the steering wheel, he wiped each palm against a pant leg. "There's a question I wanted to ask you. And I haven't known quite how to say it."

"Why does that sound ominous?"

"It's not ominous. It's just, well… It's personal. I need to know about the engagement ring Brandt proposed with. Did he tell you anything about where he got it?"

She chuckled. "He didn't know where it came from. It wasn't his ring."

Jordan started. "What?"

Her face averted, Lucy stared at the passing scenery. "The ring belonged to my great-aunt. She passed away a few years ago, and she didn't have any children. She left me her jewelry and a few other items in her estate. The rest went to my mom."

Jordan vacillated between relief and confusion. "Then he didn't buy you a ring?"

"No. Though he promised to. Everything was rushed when we got engaged, and there was no time to go shopping. I thought it was a waste of money anyway. The ring from my aunt had been sitting in a jewelry box collecting dust for years. Brandt always felt guilty about it, though. You know how he liked grand gestures."

"He wanted to propose to you properly," Jordan said, his chest constricting. "And he wanted that proposal to be special."

"That was Brandt. I'll always wonder what he had up his sleeve. Knowing him, it was something unique."

"I can shed some light on that." Jordan gathered his courage. "I've been such an idiot. I should have said something earlier."

He'd been agonizing all this time when a simple conversation would have cleared up the whole misunderstanding. Having an exact replica of the ring specially made was just the sort of thing Brandt would do. He'd obviously wanted to propose to Lucy properly while still preserving his original proposal.

Jordan had never been so grateful for a darkened car. He didn't want Lucy to read the shame in his expression.

Reaching into his pocket, he retrieved the length of embroidered blue silk, then extended his hand. "There's something inside. It's from Brandt."

After carefully unraveling the material, she revealed the ring Jordan had been carrying in his pocket for the past month.

Her breath caught. "I don't understand. How? This looks almost exactly like my aunt's ring."

"I'm sorry I didn't give it to you sooner. Brandt had it made when we were overseas. He gave it to me for safekeeping the day of the bombing. There was a mix-up at the hospital, and it's been sitting in storage for most of the year. When someone discovered the mistake, they returned it to me. I should have given it to you that first day. I wanted to, but you were wearing a ring, an identical ring. And there was a… It doesn't matter. I'm sorry."

They'd reached her house, and he pulled into

the driveway. Neither of them made a move to exit the car.

Her head bent, Lucy ran the length of delicate blue silk between her fingers. "Why didn't you tell me sooner? Why did you wait?"

He gripped the steering wheel harder. What was he supposed to say? That he'd encountered Brandt in the lobby of the hotel with a woman and something about the meeting had seemed off? That from the first moment he'd seen Lucy, he'd wanted to make her happy? That he'd wanted to ensure her happiness even if it meant preserving Brandt's memory with a lie?

Instead, he said, "I don't know. I was wrong, and I'm sorry."

"You were worried, weren't you?" She reverently held the ring between her thumb and forefinger. "You didn't know why there were two rings, and you didn't want me to think badly of him."

"He was my friend," Jordan said, his voice catching. "I never should have doubted him. There were other things. I can't tell you what they were—it's classified. But it doesn't matter. I was wrong."

Lucy rested her hand on his sleeve. "I think I understand. I'd have done the same thing in your position. I'd have tried to figure out why there was a second ring rather than risk hurting someone. That's nothing to be ashamed of."

"He loved you," Jordan said. "And he wanted to do right by you. He wanted you to be happy. He was a good man."

The truth was innocuous and logical. He'd wrapped himself in knots because he didn't want to hurt Lucy. But a part of him feared that he'd also been protecting himself. He'd wanted to preserve the memory of the three of them. He wanted to preserve the memory of listening to Brandt read Lucy's emails out loud. Of knowing that his feelings for her were safe and contained and harmless.

He'd known in his heart that he'd never be able to compete with someone like Brandt. He didn't want to spend the rest of his life being compared to Brandt and coming up short.

"He was a good man." Lucy's sigh was barely audible. "You wanted me to be happy, as well. I appreciate that. More than you know."

"This is all going to be over soon, Lucy. I promise you. I'm expecting the call saying they've apprehended the buyer anytime now."

"You know, I'm almost dreading that call," she said, pushing open her door.

"Why is that?"

"Because when this is finished, I'll have lost you both."

"You won't lose me, Lucy."

"I'll see you tomorrow."

His heart aching, he watched her walk away, then picked up his phone and dialed Mike.

"I don't think Brandt was taking bribes," Jordan said.

"What did you find out?"

"It's a long story, but he had a legitimate reason for wanting the ring made. Remember how you said the two guys from the CIA were watching the shop? Well, I doubt they were the only ones. Brandt just picked the wrong shop at the wrong time. Once he had that ring made, everyone was looking at him. Talk to those guys in the CIA. I bet the girl the jeweler mentioned was working for the other side. I saw her with Brandt in the lobby of the hotel. I knew there was something funny about the exchange. I'm guessing she was trying to seduce him. That's why he looked uncomfortable."

"Makes sense. I'll get a list of known foreign agents and let you take a look. See if you can pick out the girl."

"Thanks."

"Hey. I'm sorry. That's a tough break. Brandt was a good guy. One of the best."

"Yeah. He was."

Brandt was just a guy who was in the wrong place at the wrong time. Lucy never needed to know his visit to the jewelry shop had brought him to the attention of foreign spies. They'd thought he was taking a bribe, and when they discovered he was clean, they'd unraveled the thread. Maybe one of the workers at the hotel had seen something and slipped the information to someone for a price.

They'd probably never know exactly how their cover was blown. There was always a risk when they worked overseas. Causing Lucy more grief solved nothing.

She had the ring. She knew what was in Brandt's heart, and that was enough.

Jordan was relieved that Brandt's death would not be in vain. They had more information now. They had a path to finding the men who had organized the suicide bombing.

He'd lost his friend. With a muffled sob, he pressed his forehead against the steering wheel.

Now, after all this time, he could finally mourn him.

SEVENTEEN

Lucy sat in a cardboard lifeboat with three other employees and Jordan. There were four other identical boats, each manned with five people.

Sue stood at the head of the room. "Okay. Here's how this works. There are five people in your boat. There's a doctor with a painkiller addiction—that'll be you, Ellie. There's a married couple—that's Jordan and Lucy. She's a nurse, and he's a construction worker. They have two children. There's also a criminal—that's you, Gerry. You've been charged with murder, but you're the only one who can navigate the boat. There's also a minister—that's Tom. He's proved to be cool in a crisis and was the one who managed to get the lifeboat into the water in the first place." Sue paused for dramatic effect. "One of you must be eliminated from the boat."

Everyone in the room groaned, and Sue appeared affronted. "This will be fun. It's a test of teamwork and problem-solving."

At the expression on Jordan's face, Lucy stifled a giggle. The company held an off-site meeting after hours in the classrooms beneath the Lied Jungle at the Henry Doorly Zoo each year. The day consisted of a series of team-building events, followed by a party that included families. Normally Lucy dreaded the event, but since Jordan was compelled to attend, the day had been more than tolerable. She'd even had fun.

There'd been a few boring meetings while the CEO lectured them on how well the company was performing. The schedule was interspersed with sumo wrestling in inflatable costumes and other team-building events. This was the final challenge of the day before they were released for dinner.

Gerry, the assigned criminal, stood with a shrug. "This is easy. Guess I'll go."

He was a portly, balding man in his midsixties and the only person who dreaded this event more than Lucy.

Ellie blocked his exit. "You can't go. You're the only one who can steer the boat."

Lucy groaned. Leave it to Ellie to complicate things. If this was a cruise ship, she'd be the cruise director.

Jordan grinned at Lucy. "Hey, wife. It's a good thing we left the kids at home, considering how this is turning out."

She stuck out her tongue at him.

Gerry remained standing, and Lucy appreciated his optimism. She doubted they were getting out of this anytime soon. Not with Ellie taking charge.

"Okay," Gerry declared. "We get rid of the construction worker. We're on a boat. We don't need him."

"But what if something happens to the boat?" Ellie crossed her arms over her chest. "He might be the only one who can fix it."

"It's a boat." Gerry guffawed. "How complicated can the repairs be?"

"No." Tom shook his head. "If we live, we'll be stranded on a desert island. We'll need the construction worker to help us build the huts and the infrastructure and stuff."

Lucy's eyes widened. In a flash they'd gone from surviving at sea to building huts.

"Then let's get rid of the clergy guy," Gerry offered. "What's he adding?"

Ellie gasped. "You can't throw a clergyman off the boat. He was the one who got us on the boat in the first place. We'll need spiritual guidance if we're going to create an island nation."

An island nation? Lucy gaped. They were

never going to be done in time for dinner at this rate, and she was starving.

"All right, all right." Tom flapped his hands. "If I'm a clergyman, then I understand sacrifice. I'll throw myself off. Problem solved."

"Didn't you hear what I just said?" Ellie huffed. "We'll need you for spiritual guidance."

Lucy exchanged a glance with Jordan. His shoulders shook with laughter, and he covered his face.

"Fine." Gerry threw back his head and arms like a toddler having a fit in the supermarket. "Then who should stay? Maybe we should start there? Once we decide who stays, we'll know who has to go."

"I say we keep the nurse," Tom stated confidently. "We might need medical attention. And we should keep the guy who can steer the boat."

Gerry smirked. "Yeah. If we can't steer, we'll just be floating out here in circles forever."

"And he's not likely to teach anyone else how, is he?" Ellie glared at Gerry as though he'd actually been accused of a crime. "He's a criminal—he's not stupid. He'll know you're just going to throw him overboard once you don't need him anymore."

"But how do we know he's really a murderer?" Tom interjected. "Sue just said he was *charged* with murder. She didn't say he was guilty. What if he's innocent and we vote an innocent man off the boat?"

Of all the team-building exercises she'd been involved in over the years, this was turning out to be Lucy's favorite.

Gerry stood up again. "This is a trick. I know it. We should all go down together. All for one and one for all."

He pumped his fist to drive the point home.

Clipboard in hand, Sue appeared at the side of the "boat." "You can't all go down with the ship. The game says you have to decide who should stay and who should go."

Lucy turned to Jordan. "What do you think? Who would you choose?"

If she didn't get some food soon, she was going to punch a hole in the bottom of the boat no matter what the rules said.

Jordan assumed a serious expression. "I say we join forces and rebel against Sue. She's the one who made the rules. If we overthrow her, we can do what we want. Then we can change the rules and everyone gets to stay on the boat."

Sue threw up her papers with a laugh and they fluttered over her. "I declare team five the winner."

The entire conference room erupted in cheers. Lucy half expected them to hoist Jordan on their shoulders and carry him to dinner. Thankfully, they settled for slapping him on the back and offering hearty congratulations.

Then everyone melted away and they were face-to-face once again. As though they'd come full circle from that first day, they exchanged an awkward hug.

Lucy tucked a strand of hair behind her ear. "Thank you. I thought our boat was going to erupt in mutiny and we'd all be dead."

Jordan grinned. He started to say something, but his phone buzzed. He glanced at the screen and his expression sobered. "Westover is waiting outside. He has news for us."

Her smile faded. She'd known the end of their time was near—she just wasn't prepared for it to come this soon.

Jordan's features were leaden, and Lucy appeared equally reluctant to meet with Westover. They should be happy. This was the culmination of everything they'd worked for. Jordan had no doubt Westover had come to deliver the news they were all waiting for.

The agent was waiting for them at the entrance of the zoo. "Karp says we got a hit on the drone software," he stated without preamble. "Looks like someone uploaded the code and took one of the Afghanistan drones for a joyride. He snapped a few pictures and sent it back to home base."

"Nothing else?" Jordan asked, his heart sinking.

He'd spent his last evening with Lucy arguing about survivors on a fake lifeboat. Not exactly an auspicious parting.

"Lucy's code worked like a charm." Westover practically vibrated with excitement. "The drone reported the location of the controller back to the mainframe, and then went into safety mode. The whole thing was monitored remotely in case he decided to deploy a missile. He didn't. This means we're golden. The NSA team will give him twenty-four hours to feel comfortable, and then we'll send in an extraction team."

"That's great," Lucy said, her voice flat.

Westover flipped back his coat and planted his hands on his hips. "You haven't even heard the best part. We were right. This guy is local."

Jordan frowned. "Seems almost too easy."

"I'll take easy," Westover declared. "But don't rest on your laurels. We're not finished with this thing yet. We still don't have the identity of the seller, the one who originally impersonated Lucy. Keep your eyes open. I want them both."

Lucy touched Jordan's sleeve. "I have to go. I told Sue I'd help pass out the cake with dinner."

"Sure thing," he replied, watching her walk away.

A low whistle startled him.

"Earth to Harris," Westover prodded.

"What? Oh." Jordan brushed his troubled thoughts aside. "Are you sticking around? I'd like backup until this guy is in custody."

"Yeah. Karp doesn't want Lucy spending too much time alone until the buyer is in custody." Westover patted his stomach. "Think I'll grab something to eat while I'm here. You coming?"

"You go ahead. I'll be along in a minute."

Jordan was lost in thought when his phone buzzed again. His stepsister, Emma, had sent him a text along with a photo attachment.

As he read the message, pressure built behind his eyes.

You're an uncle! It's a girl!

She posed with the baby and her husband, Liam. She looked radiant. Happier than he'd ever seen her, and remorse sucked the air from his lungs.

He loved Lucy, but he'd been too afraid of being compared to Brandt and falling short to act on his feelings. Sure, he'd told himself it was about loyalty and all that. In truth, he was scared. Now was the time for courage. He'd rather spend the rest of his life coming up short if he got to spend that time with Lucy.

Had his realization come too late? Since their lunch meeting, she'd been distant. Not that he was surprised. He'd driven her away, and he had only himself to blame. If what Westover said was true, and the situation in the Middle East was heating up, he didn't have the time he needed to mend his bridges.

He'd gone and made a real mess out of things.

He loved Lucy and he'd done everything in his power to drive her away.

Lucy sipped her iced tea and casually searched the crowd. Westover's news was brilliant. They'd found the buyer. Her plan had worked. She blinked rapidly. This was good. The sooner Jordan returned home, the sooner she could start rebuilding her life. She'd done it before, so there was no reason she couldn't do it again.

A soda clutched in each hand, Sue glided over. "There you are! I've been looking for you everywhere. Jordan is doing a sweep of the conference rooms to make sure we didn't leave anything behind. You should take pity on him and help him out."

Sue was still trying to play matchmaker, and Lucy didn't have the heart to tell her the effort was wasted. "They always make the new guy do that. I should have warned him."

"Thank you. I've got to run. I'm hiding from Ellie. She's miffed about the lifeboat challenge and won't shut up. She wanted to vote you off, by the way."

"I was the nurse! She'd have died on that desert island without me."

Sue giggled. "Don't forget about Jordan. If you need me, I'll be as far away from Ellie as possible."

Grateful for something to do besides mope, Lucy returned to the jungle once more. She was about to take the stairs down to the lower-level conference rooms when movement caught the corner of her eye. Vance Eagan was making his way down the corridor toward the entrance of the jungle.

Why on earth was he doing that? They'd all been told more than once that the exhibits were closed once dinner was served. She started to follow, then paused. Maybe he was meeting Emily. The last thing she wanted to do was interrupt a tryst.

Lucy crossed to the large glass windows and searched the crowd. Emily was returning from the buffet line, her plate laden with food. Lucy didn't know why Vance was entering the jungle exhibit, but she might as well warn him that he was going to run afoul of the zoo authorities.

The cavernous indoor jungle had both an upper level and a lower level, and Vance had been going down the stairs, so that was where she started her search. The moment she pressed open the door, the humidity hit her like a wall. Pausing a moment, she acclimated to the thick air.

The first floor of the exhibit was a dirt-packed jungle path that wound through the trees and over a meandering stream. While the monkeys and the other mammals and reptiles were safely enclosed in their exhibits, the birds and the bats were left to roam freely.

Though she wasn't supposed to be here either, Lucy couldn't help but enjoy the solitude. Normally the popular attraction was crushed with visitors. Catching herself, she pressed forward. This wasn't a sightseeing tour.

The path took a sharp curve, and she heard a muffled shriek followed by a hushed admonishing.

"Be quiet, Connie." Vance's words were muffled, as though he was speaking through clenched teeth. "What's going on? We're not supposed to be in this exhibit once dinner starts."

"Who's gonna tell?" a female voice demanded. "The monkeys?"

"Why are you here in the first place? You can't be seen at work events. We talked about this."

The two hadn't seen or heard Lucy, which gave her an advantage. Birds called and water rushed over a two-story waterfall, masking her footsteps as she crept along the path. Dense foliage on each side provided good cover.

Keeping her body positioned behind a large tree, Lucy peered around the trunk. Vance was speaking with a woman who bore a remarkable resemblance to Lucy. She was at least ten years older, but the height and the build were almost identical. With a wig and the proper clothing, she'd be an excellent match on the security cameras.

Her heart hammering against her ribs, Lucy pulled out her phone and texted Jordan to meet her in the jungle exhibit.

Something scuttled along the ground next to Lucy, and Vance spun around. He stared right at her. As recognition dawned, a flush spread up his neck.

He quickly cycled through several expressions as though deciding how he wanted to spin his explanation.

"Oh, hey, Lucy," he called cheerfully. "We

were just leaving. The exhibits are closed, so you better leave, too."

Acting as though she hadn't noticed anything amiss, Lucy strolled down the path until she stood directly before them. Neither Vance nor the woman looked like much of a threat, and as long as they didn't suspect she knew anything, they weren't likely to harm her anyway. She wanted to stall them until Jordan arrived. He'd know what to do.

A dark shape swooped over them, and Connie shrieked.

Lucy shuddered. A bat. She caught sight of a basket of hanging fruit near the second level. With all the visitors gone, it was feeding time, and the bats were active. They soared overhead, plunging and challenging each other for their dinner.

Lucy assumed a cheerful expression to match Vance's. "Aren't you going to introduce me? Who's this?"

"Oh, uh." Vance's face flamed with color. "This is my sister, Connie. Connie, this is Lucy. From work."

"Nice to meet you, Connie." Anger built in Lucy's chest. Jordan was on his way and Vance looked as though he might collapse at any moment. These two had played with her life. They'd nearly destroyed her reputation. They might have gotten her killed. She really wasn't in the mood to play nice. "When did you decide to set me up?"

Vance flashed his palms as though he was defending himself from an attack. "I don't know what you're talking about."

"Sure you do," Lucy said easily. "You can play dumb if you want, but now that we know it was you, it's not going to take us long to find enough evidence to charge you with treason."

"Evidence of what?" Vance demanded. Since the friendly act wasn't working, he reverted to bluster. A classic move from a liar. "You're just a low-level programmer. You don't know anything about what happens in that company."

"I know more than you think." Lucy held up her phone. Vance was a blusterer and bully, but he wasn't dangerous. She'd dealt with his kind before. He'd waste his breath defending himself. "For example, I know the NSA has been working undercover in the office for weeks. It's over."

The blood drained from Connie's face and she backed away. "It was all Vance's idea. I didn't want nothing to do with it."

Vance spun toward her. "Connie!"

"Nuh-uh. No way. I'm not going to jail over this. You said the plan was foolproof."

"Keep your mouth shut," Vance ordered.

"No. I'm not going to keep my mouth shut. I haven't gotten any of the money you promised, and that guy said he already paid us the diamonds and he isn't paying us any more."

"Wait." Lucy stepped between them. "What guy?"

"The guy we made the deal with. He didn't pay us."

Vance made a guttural sound deep in his throat. "He didn't pay us because you can't follow instructions. I gave you the password. I gave you the instructions. I gave you everything and you still got locked out of the system. If you had just done what I asked, we'd be rich and they'd all be blaming Lucy."

Despite his bravado, Vance recognized that there was no escaping. Connie had been caught, and she was like a drowning woman—she was going to take everyone down with her.

Connie sneered at her brother. "Well, you must have made a mistake, because I followed your instructions exactly, and they didn't work."

Lucy snapped her fingers. "Enough."

The two went silent and stared at her. Connie had mentioned the diamonds, and that had Lucy concerned.

"What do you know about this guy who offered to buy the code for the drones?" Lucy asked.

Vance glanced at Connie and back again. Lucy figured he was trying to decide how much the information was worth. He probably wanted to bargain for a better deal when they sent him to prison.

"I don't know anything about the buyer. I never met him in person. He was sniffing around some of the coding message boards. There were rumors he'd pay top dollar for the right information." His voice took on a nasal whine. "I haven't gotten a raise in two years. This company owes me. If they don't want to pay me, then I decided to get my money elsewhere. I made up a false profile, and I had Connie pretend she was you. He didn't suspect a thing. You were an employee, after all. It was foolproof."

The two of them glanced at Connie. She was the one weak link in the chain. If she'd gotten into the secure files, they might have succeeded in fooling everyone.

"What happened after he gave you the down payment?" Lucy asked, stalling for time until Jordan arrived.

She glanced at her phone, but he hadn't replied. The jungle was clammy, and a fine bead of sweat traced a path down her cheek. Instead of letting her anger get the better of her, she should have waited for Jordan. She'd expected him to storm in by now.

"This is your fault." Vance glared at Connie. "You got locked out of the system and suddenly the company security was going nuts and looking at everybody."

"Me," Lucy interjected. "They were looking at *me*!"

"Yeah. But you didn't do it. And nothing happened. No harm. No foul. The guy didn't know who I was anyway. So I just ghosted him. Stopped answering his texts. I'd already gotten a down payment—I didn't want to go to jail."

"Yeah," Lucy said. "Except your buyer thought he was dealing with me, and he found me. Remember that coffee shop shooting last month? That was meant for me. Or, rather, meant for the person the buyer thought had reneged on the deal."

Vance shook his head. "That's not my fault. I figured… I figured…"

"Never mind." She gritted her teeth. "Why use your own computer? That's the one thing that confuses me."

Where was Jordan? If he didn't appear soon, she was going to have to find a way to extract herself. Sooner or later these two were going to realize that no one was coming.

Vance appeared almost cocky. "I used my

computer because the best place to hide is in plain sight."

This was getting Lucy nowhere, so she turned to Connie. "When did the buyer talk to you about the diamonds?"

"Tonight."

Both Lucy and Vance turned their shocked attention on her. "What do you mean, tonight?"

"I contacted him. I told him we could still make a deal. He's meeting us here. That's what I've been trying to tell you."

Vance snatched her arm. "Then he knows we're here? He knows where to find us?"

Lucy's stomach dropped. They were sitting ducks.

The next instant, the cavernous space plunged into darkness.

Jordan stared at his phone in horror. Six minutes. Lucy had sent the text six minutes before.

He sprinted the distance to the jungle and ripped open the door to a midnight-black wall of humidity.

This wasn't right. There were emergency lights. Someone must have cut the power to both the main circuits and the backup generator.

His adrenaline spiked.

Since he didn't know what he was going to find inside, Jordan kept the screen on his phone covered. There was no use making himself a target. He'd been through the exhibit earlier in the day, but he hadn't exactly memorized the path. The foliage was dense, and if he kept to the clear spaces, he should be able to navigate fairly easily.

Something moved to Jordan's left. Stalking through the pitch darkness, he strained his ears. Animal sounds and rushing water camouflaged anything else he might have heard.

Hushed voices sounded to his left. He inched his way over the uneven terrain and caught the faint outline of two figures.

A twig snapped beneath his feet.

The man whipped around and Jordan recognized Vance, an employee from Consolidated Unlimited.

Jordan snatched his arm. Vance shrieked and clawed at the restraint.

"Stop it," Jordan whispered harshly. "It's me. Jordan Harris. Where's Lucy?"

"I don't know." The struggles ceased. "Look, I don't know what's going on here. I came in here and the lights went out. That's all I know."

Vance was lying through his teeth.

Jordan shone the light from his phone toward the second figure. She was older, but the size and build were an exact match for Lucy. His heart thudded against his ribs. They had their impostor. They had the buyer. They had everything.

He had everything but Lucy.

No wonder she'd told him to meet her here. She must have seen Vance with the woman and put two and two together.

"Where's Lucy?" Jordan demanded again.

"I don't know." Vance shook his head. "I don't know anything. I came here and the lights went out. That's all I know."

"Don't lie to me, Vance. You're only digging the hole deeper for yourself."

"Don't be an idiot, Vance," the woman declared. "They know everything. You're not fooling anybody, and you're going to get us all killed. He's here. The buyer is in the building. I think he grabbed Lucy when the lights went out."

"You two get out of here," Jordan ordered. "We'll discuss this later."

They were deadweight and they couldn't run far. Right now, he didn't need the distraction.

The fear that had started low in his belly was threatening to choke him. The buyer had Lucy. If he'd come out of hiding, then he was desperate.

Desperate men were dangerous.

Jordan texted Westover and requested backup from the local law enforcement. The jungle had two levels and an exit on each. He texted Westover again and instructed him to watch the doors on the lower floor while he made his way to the upper level.

This guy was bold. He wasn't going to sneak out like a whipped dog. He'd likely walked in through the front right under the nose of security. He'd probably walk out the same way.

It was a gamble, but Jordan exited the floor of the jungle and crept up the stairs to the second level.

He needed the element of surprise.

Once on the second level, he reached for his phone and dialed Lucy's number.

Sure enough, the faint strains of a ringtone echoed from just to his left.

"It's over," Jordan hollered. "The police are on their way."

"I've got a gun on her."

Jordan's pulse stalled before he got ahold of himself. *Focus on the mission.* That was the most important goal.

"You're not going to get out of here," he called. A faint ambient light illuminated dark shapes. "Let's talk this out before somebody gets hurt."

"Not gonna happen. I've got the girl. If you want her to live, you're going to find a way to make sure I walk out that door without anything happening to me."

"I don't know how I'm going to do that."

"You'll think of something."

Jordan cocked his head and reached for his gun. "Do you hear that? It's sirens. This place is going to be swarmed in about two minutes. If you want to come out of this alive, you'll have to make a deal with me."

"You're not listening. I got duped. Twice. I'm not getting duped again."

"Then why are you here?"

Jordan used the echoes from the man's voice to track his position. Keeping low, he crept forward.

"Imagine my surprise when, just as I was about to sell the code to the highest bidder, I received a rather curious text. Ms. Sutton was contacting me to let me know she was ready to provide the information I'd requested. You can imagine my confusion. Out of curiosity, I went along with her. It didn't take long to realize there were two Lucys, and they were both playing me for a fool. I asked for a meeting, and she walked right into a trap. Lucky me, I got two for the price of one."

It was odd, both of them calling to each other in the darkness, each competing with the animal calls and the sound of running water. Judging by the changes in his speech volume, Vance was on the move. He wasn't navigating toward the exit. Instead, he was moving farther along the path.

Though Jordan had the man holding Lucy trapped, he wouldn't relax. There was always a chance the guy knew of an alternate exit. He was a local, after all. He'd known about the back exit in the park. It didn't take a big leap of faith to infer he might know an alternate exit from this building.

"Jordan," Lucy called.

His heart lodged in his throat.

She yelped and went silent.

Jordan's blood boiled. "What did you do?"

"I've encouraged her to be silent."

Jordan glanced at the clock on his phone. At least four minutes had passed. Backup should be here by now.

Then again, the guy holding Lucy should know that, as well. Had Jordan been stalling the buyer, or had the buyer been stalling him? He didn't trust this guy.

"Come now," the man called. "You haven't told me how you're going to get us out of the situation. You're a smart guy."

A flashing red light caught Jordan's attention. The guy had obviously cut the power to the main building and also the backup generators, but the fire alarm was wired separately.

Aiming his gun above their estimated location, Jordan yanked on the fire alarm. His action triggered the alarm and emergency floodlights marking all the exits.

Lucy and the man were barely fifteen feet ahead of him.

The man yanked Lucy backward and she stumbled.

A dark form swooped from the ceiling and flew in front of the pair.

The man flailed his arms. He was having difficulty holding on to Lucy and the gun while keeping his attention trained on Jordan.

His heart racing, Jordan calculated his shot.

He told himself not to look at Lucy, but at the last instant, he couldn't help himself. He met her steady gaze. She didn't appear frightened—only resigned.

She glanced down and he followed her gaze.

She lifted her booted foot a fraction.

They didn't need words. He knew exactly what she was about to do.

The moment she stomped, the buyer howled in pain. Lucy jerked away and Jordan fired.

The man collapsed, one arm reaching for Lucy, but she'd already danced away, out of his reach.

Westover appeared a second later, and the next instant, the entire building was swarmed with police officers.

Jordan scooped Lucy into his arms and held her like he'd never let go.

She burrowed against his chest. "Please, please, please tell me this is the last time we will be surrounded by police officers like this."

"I promise."

He rocked her and held her close. Though he wanted to shout his love from the rooftops, this was not the time or place.

"I want to go home."

Jordan held her close. "Then that's where I'll take you."

He'd been afraid all this time. He'd been afraid to trust his feelings. Afraid he was a poor substitute for the man she'd lost. He'd been afraid to let go of the guilt. He was no longer going to let the fear and misplaced shame keep him from God. He sure wasn't going to let those emotions keep him from loving Lucy.

Even if she no longer wanted him, at least he'd know he'd given her his heart.

Lucy woke on her couch to find Jordan asleep on the chair across from her. She sat up and brushed the mass of hair from her forehead.

The movement woke him, and he blinked sleepily.

"You're here," she exclaimed in wonder.

He flushed and rubbed at the stubble on his chin. "I didn't want to leave you alone. Oh, and I fed your guinea pig. Don't let him tell you otherwise. He was gunning for a second carrot from me."

Her eyes burned. If she hadn't been certain before, his action had cemented her feelings.

There was absolutely no doubt in her mind that she loved this man. "Thank you. For everything."

"I wouldn't be any place other than where you needed me."

He'd swept her away from the lights and the sirens last evening, and he'd driven her home, where she'd cried herself to sleep in his arms.

For the rest of her life, she never wanted to be a part of another crime scene. "Who was he, anyway? The buyer?"

"His name is actually John Dobbs. Such an ordinary name. Kind of a letdown considering the guy caused us so many problems."

"Is he dead?"

She'd heard the gunshot and she'd seen the blood. The rest was a blur.

"He's alive. He'll survive. He's already talking, too. For all his cloak-and-dagger nonsense, he's a coward at heart. While I don't condone

Vance or Connie's actions, they turned out to be John's undoing. He'd run the scam twice before with perfect results. He had what he thought was a reliable system. He'd make a deal for the information and offer a generous down payment. Then he'd pay for the information in diamonds. Once he got what he wanted, he'd hack his mark's bank account and steal whatever money they'd gotten from the diamonds."

"That's diabolical."

"Yep. Because who's going to turn themselves in? What were they going to say once the authorities started looking into their accounts? They couldn't risk having anyone ask questions. So they stayed quiet."

"What about the cemetery? He killed someone."

"Doesn't look like he did. Near as we can tell, they all knew each other as kids. They were called Triple J because all their names began with the same letter. John hired Jigsaw and Jimmy to put pressure on you, but they went off script. When things got violent, John refused to pay. That's when Jigsaw and Jimmy got into a fight. Jimmy got off the first shot, but he missed. Jigsaw didn't."

"Then Jigsaw lied to us. He said someone had put a price on his head."

"All of that was a fabrication. He knew he was

going down for something, and he figured the kidnapping charges were better than murder."

Dazed, Lucy sat back on the couch. "I thought he was going to be a supervillain or something. But he was just an average joe. A greedy average joe who wasn't opposed to blackmail."

"And in way over his head. Probably good that we got to him first. He was dealing with some dangerous people."

"Thank you. For saving me."

"I would have gotten there sooner, but I didn't see your text right away. Sue had me cornered. She was singing your praises and wondering why I hadn't asked you out on a date. I think maybe she'd gotten an extra drink ticket from someone, because she was very forceful."

"I'm sorry. She's been saying the same things to me for weeks."

Jordan sucked in a breath. "Lucy, I—"

She held up her hand. "I know, you want to be friends."

"No. I don't think we can ever be friends."

Lucy glanced up sharply. "Oh?"

"I'm in love with you."

"Oh, Jordan."

"I don't know if you can ever love me. I'll understand if you can't. I'm nothing like Brandt. I don't have his personality. I'm never going to be like him."

"I don't want you to be like him." Lucy slipped off the couch and knelt before him, taking his hands in her own. "I loved Brandt. I'll always love Brandt. But I need you. I ache for you."

"What are you saying?" he asked, his voice choked with emotion.

"I love you," Lucy said, staring into his eyes. "I think I loved you from the moment you gave Mr. Nibbles a handful of carrots even after he bit you."

"It wasn't a very hard bite."

"Yes, but I knew then what kind of man you are."

"I feel so guilty. He should be here. I didn't want to feel like I was living another man's life."

"How do you think I felt? I found a once-in-a-lifetime love…twice." She rubbed the sleep from her eyes. She must look awful, but she didn't care. "Brandt would want us to be happy. I like to think there was a part of his spirit that brought us together. I've been lost until I found you. Every moment of life is precious. We're alive and every second is a gift."

"You have to know what you're getting into. I want a house together. The kids. Everything. I want love. Real love. The terrifying kind of love where you feel like you're falling and you'll never hit the bottom. I'm not perfect—"

"Stop." She pressed two fingers against his

lips. "None of that talk. I want you. Just the way you are." She wrapped her arms around him and held him close. "All I want is you. We're perfect together."

His lips found hers. It was a kiss of discovery and a kiss of freedom. They'd freed each other from the past. Her soul thrilled at his caress, and as he slid his fingers into her hair, she pressed closer.

Pulling away, he studied her. "I love those blue highlights. I love you."

"I love you, too."

EPILOGUE

Six months later

Lucy was putting the finishing touches on the buffet for her combination engagement and going-away party when her mom arrived.

Vicky Sutton breezed into the kitchen and took in the chaos. Her expression fell, and her precisely styled hair seemed to droop.

"Really, Lucy." Her mom touched her shoulder. "You have got to do something about this."

Because today was special, Lucy had worn an ivory A-line dress with lace-up boots. She'd added a few more blue highlights, as well, since Jordan seemed to like them.

"No, Mom. I don't," she said, stepping away.

"Oh, well, if you don't want to be taken seriously, that's no skin off my nose."

Lucy steeled her nerves. "Mom, you've got to stop."

"Stop what?"

"Stop trying to make me something different. I'm not going to change. This is the way I am, and I wish you'd accept that."

Her mom huffed. "I'm only trying to help. You might have a little gratitude."

"You might be trying to help, but you're not. You want everything to be neat and tidy and ordered, and I'm never going to be those things. I'm messy. I make mistakes. You need everything neat and I'm not neat."

"Are you saying that's my fault? I raised you alone, and I did the best I could."

"It's not your fault," Lucy said, recognizing the guilt her mom felt. "You did a great job raising me. Now it's time to stop. This is who I am."

"It's hard to stop. Someday, when you're a mother, you'll understand."

"And when that happens, I'll have you to guide me."

"I'm going to miss you." Her mom's eyes filled with tears. "Do you have to move all the way to Maryland?"

"It's a wonderful opportunity. I thought you wanted me to move out of the neighborhood and get a better job?"

"Yes, but not for a man. What if you follow him out there and he dumps you?"

Lucy suppressed a smile. "That's not going to happen."

"I guess this is how it feels, isn't it?"

"How what feels?"

"When someone makes a decision and doesn't include you."

"Yes, Mom, that's how it feels. It's not a bad thing, you know. You gave me independence."

Jordan lumbered into the kitchen carrying two enormous bags of ice. "Good to see you, Mrs. Sutton. I was hoping to speak to you privately."

Her mom's eyebrows shot up her forehead. "All right."

Lucy smiled. She never doubted that Jordan had courage, because facing her mom was going to require all of his fortitude.

Soon the house and the yard were overflowing with people. There was laughter and food, and though Lucy felt a tug of sadness that she was leaving this behind, she was excited for the future.

At precisely four o'clock, Jordan found her and hugged her around the waist.

She tipped back her head and kissed him. "How did my mom take it?"

"Like a champ."

"Speech, speech," someone shouted.

Jordan took her hand. They stood together on the low stone wall that surrounded her garden.

He cleared his throat. "I'd like to thank you

all for coming. As you all know, this is a combination party. Lucy and I have gotten engaged, and she's taken a job in Washington. Since you all know Lucy, you know that she has her own unique way of doing things. That's why tonight we're not only celebrating our engagement—we're getting married."

A shocked gasp erupted from the crowd, followed by a raucous cheer.

"If everyone will meet us in the backyard in ten minutes, we're going to hold the ceremony there."

Excited chatter flowed through their guests. Lucy's mom took charge of the crowd, guiding everyone through to where the ceremony was about to take place. Pressure built behind Lucy's eyes. Jordan was right—her mom had taken the surprise like a champ.

Twenty minutes later, she and Jordan stood before their friends and family and exchanged the vows they'd written themselves.

"Lucy Sutton, I promise to always bring Mr. Nibbles carrots even if he bites me," Jordan declared.

Lucy teared up. "You said his name in front of people."

"Yes." He smiled. They were both focused on each other and oblivious to the crowd behind them. "But can we name your next pet something different? Like Spike or Fido?"

"Of course."

The minister heaved a long-suffering sigh. "Shall we continue the ceremony?"

"Yes." Lucy held her bouquet of daisies in front of her smile. "We can continue. Jordan Harris, I promise to always be the Rogue to your Gambit."

Tears welled in his eyes. "You know my favorite superheroes."

She wasn't only gaining a husband; she was gaining an entire comic book collection. "Of course I know your favorite superheroes."

When the minister pronounced them husband and wife, their friends and family cheered. Her heart brimming with love, she threaded her fingers through his, and they turned and faced their future. Together.

* * * * *

Dear Reader,

Thank you for reading *Stolen Secrets*! For this story, I wanted to explore both the grieving process and how life changes after the death of a loved one. While most of us are familiar with the five stages of grief, we often don't think about what follows the acceptance phase. Lucy and Jordan were both hesitant to move on with their lives. Because of that uncertainty, they were both stuck.

Together they learned that moving on doesn't mean forgetting or even letting go of the grief entirely. Instead, they each made the decision to invest their love and emotion in healthy, life-affirming relationships.

I love connecting with readers and would love to hear your thoughts on this story! If you're interested in learning more about this book—or other books and series I have written—I have more information on my website: sherrishackelford.com. I can also be reached by email at sherri@sherrishackelford.com, and snail mail, PO Box 116, Elkhorn, NE, 68022.

Happy Reading!
Sherri Shackelford